Bodhi
Gets the Blues

Anand Am Reet

Bodhi Gets the Blues

Book One of the Bodhi Dharma Series

Bodhi Dharma is a fictional character and not related to the historical Bodhidharma. See Author's note.

ISBNs
Hardcover: 979-8-9930582-4-5
Paperback: 979-8-9930582-5-2

Printed in the United States of America

For permissions or inquiries, contact:
anandamreet@aume-buddhism.org

A Note on the Name

This story is fiction. My Bodhi Dharma is a thirteen-year-old kid with a guitar in his hands and kung fu on his mind. But Bodhidharma was also the name of a real monk, and his story has echoed through history for more than fifteen hundred years.

He came from India and made a long journey to China, crossing mountains and rivers. People say he brought a way of practicing Buddhism that focused on meditation, on sitting still, and on finding truth beyond words. In China, this grew into what became Chan Buddhism, which later spread to Japan and the world as Zen.

Legends swirl around him, the way music does around a great band. One says he meditated in a cave for nine years, sitting so still that he left a shadow on the rock. Another says he visited the Shaolin Temple and taught monks exercises to build strength, which became connected to kung fu.

And then there's the tea story. People say when his eyelids dropped to the ground, tea plants grew. The monks discovered the leaves helped them stay awake during meditation. True or not, it shows how much people admired his discipline.

My Bodhi doesn't meditate in caves. He wrestles with middle school, music, kung fu lessons, and growing up. But if his name sparks your curiosity, check out more about Bodhidharma here:
https://en.wikipedia.org/wiki/Bodhidharma

Table of Contents

Table of Contents *(Continued)*

Author's Note

When I started writing *Bodhi Gets the Blues*, I wanted it to be more than just a story about moving to a new town. Music is at the heart of this book, the way it connects people, the way it carries history, and the way it can help a kid like Bodhi make sense of the world.

The blues is real history. It grew out of struggle, survival, and hope. Many of the musicians mentioned in this book, like B.B. King, Robert Johnson, and Muddy Waters, were real people who shaped American music. Their songs influenced rock bands you may already know, like Led Zeppelin, The Rolling Stones, and Cream. I've done my best to honor their legacy while also telling a fun, fictional story about a boy learning how to find his own sound.

You'll also notice references to Buddhism, Kung Fu, and Chinese American culture. These are part of Bodhi's family life and identity. They're included here with care and respect, drawn from real traditions and teachings.

At the back of this book, you'll find two sections:

- A Bibliography, listing the professional sources I used while researching the history of the blues, Buddhism, and kung fu.
- A Further Reading & Listening section, written in Bodhi's voice, with ideas for songs, books, and history you might want to explore on your own.

Chapter 1
Call from Dad

"TURN IT DOWN!"

Sid was standing there, six years old and bossy as ever, waving his arms with the phone in his hand.

"Take those things off!" he said.

I yanked out my earbuds and grabbed the phone.

"Oh, hi Dad."

"I'm okay. Yeah, we just got in yesterday. Twin Lakes. It's a town outside Dallas. Smaller than Oceanside, but bigger than I expected. Lots of trees, trails, and, well… two lakes. Go figure.."

"Where are you?"

"Prague? Cool. How's the star?"

"Oh. Not like the old days, huh?"

Dad started as a roadie when he was young. Back then you could hang with the band after the show. Everyone together. No bodyguards with headsets. No black vans waiting at the curb. He says those nights felt like family.

He worked for Simple Minds first, since they're from Scotland like him. After that it was bands like Duran Duran, The Cure, INXS, U2, R.E.M., Oasis.

In the nineties the music got louder and messier with Nirvana and Pearl Jam. Dad says he picked up something from every tour, even if it was just how to keep a mic stand from falling over mid-song.

That's how it happened. Little lessons stacked up until one day he wasn't just the guy wrapping cables anymore. He was the one running rehearsals, pulling the pieces together, keeping the whole show stitched tight. Now he's the Music Director for a big star. We never say the name. Just "the star."

"Yeah, Sid is fine," I told him.

My brother is six. I think he's young enough not to care about moving. On the drive he had his nose buried in a stack of Pokémon cards, trading with himself since there was no one else in the backseat. When he looked up, it was only to build Lego fortresses on the seat tray and defend them against imaginary invaders. Sid doesn't just move to a new place, he rebuilds it in his head.

"Long," I said. "The drive was long. Texas is huge, space and then more space. Longhorns and windmills, over and over, like someone hit repeat on the scenery."

He asked what I was working on.

"I don't know… guitar, mostly. I played on the drive here. But it feels weird since I left the group in Oceanside."

We lived in Oceanside, California, before Mom moved us here.

Why did we move? That's the question everybody asks, so I'll just tell you. Mom said Oceanside was too much. Too many distractions, too many ways to get into trouble. Surfing, skating, late nights at the beach, kids who didn't care about school. She thought Twin Lakes, Texas would be calmer, like starting over clean. I didn't exactly get a vote.

She's renting the house in Oceanside, so maybe we can go back someday. She says no, though.

Back in Oceanside, I played in a band. Well, sort of. More like a group of kids making noise in a garage and calling it a band. We spent more time arguing about what songs to cover than actually playing them. Robbie wanted Green

Day, Ollie swore it had to be Foo Fighters, and I just wanted us to get through one whole song without falling apart.

One time we played so loud the neighbor called Animal Control because they thought something was dying in the garage. The van showed up, lights flashing. The officers searched the yard with flashlights before we convinced them it was just us.

That's when I cracked, "Every great band must first sound like a dying cat."

Dad laughed when I told him later and said, "That sounds like something an old monk would say". My Dad nicknamed me 'the old Monk' for the stuff I would come up with that sometimes sounded Zen-like and sometimes were funny. I'll be honest, sometimes they make no sense at all.

We laughed so hard about it that for a whole afternoon we were ready to rename the band *The Dead Cats.* Mom vetoed it instantly. She said nobody wants to buy tickets to hear 'dead cats'. She was probably right.

But that was us. Messy, loud, and ours. And now it's gone.

Dad plays every instrument you can think of. Guitar, drums, bass, keys. He was never famous, but he was good enough to learn from some of the best. A guitar guy from Big Country showed him fingerpicking. A drummer from The Cure taught him how to count in quietly so nobody else noticed. A keyboard tech from Depeche Mode let him sit in during soundcheck.

He never made it to the big stage, but he's pretty good. Good enough that when he picks something up, you can hear all those little lessons tucked inside. That's the thing about Dad, he collects knowledge like guitar picks. Loses some, pockets others, but always has one ready when you need it.

"Mom? She's glad to be here."

"Yeah, she talked about looking to volunteer here in Texas."

Mom is always volunteering. Food drives, beach cleanups, neighborhood meetings. If something needs doing, she shows up. She says it's part of her practice. She's an Aumé-Buddhist. So is Dad, technically, but he's more about the music and less about the volunteering.

Yes, that's how we got our names. Bodhi and Sid.

And it gets worse. My full name is Bodhi Dharma. I don't think it's Scottish. Must have been Dad being Buddhist or something. Back when he first started touring, the other roadies joked about it and started calling him "Scotty Dharma," since he was the Scottish guy always reading Zen books. He liked it, and when he became a U.S. citizen, Dharma stuck as our last name.

Where did my first name come from? Bodhi? I was named after a tree. No, really. The Bodhi Tree. That's the one the Buddha sat under until he reached enlightenment. Mom says it means "awakening."

Names are supposed to tell you who you are. Mine feels more like a riddle. An expectation I'm supposed to live up to. Try being twelve with that name.

And Sid? That's short for Siddhartha, the name of the prince who became the Buddha. Dad says it's about remembering that even regular people can change the world. Sid doesn't really think about it like that. He just says his name makes him sound older than six, which is why he prefers Sid.

"Yeah, I'm bumming. Missing the old crew. Missing the band."

"The blues, I guess."

"What do you mean? Who?"

Dad started naming names. B.B. King. Muddy Waters. Howlin' Wolf. Robert Johnson. John Lee Hooker. Then the ones who came later, like Eric Clapton and Jimi Hendrix. He said without those guys, there'd be no Led Zeppelin, no Cream, no Rolling Stones, basically half the music I love wouldn't even exist.

That's Dad. Always turning everything into a lesson. Back in Oceanside he would recommend I watch guitar lesson videos: first one chord, then two. Scales, licks, riffs. Now it's history. He says if I want to understand rock, I have to start with the blues.

So I guess that's my homework. Not math or science, but finding out why the blues mattered so much. Why those names keep echoing through the music I already love.

I guess he thinks it's funny. I got the blue because we moved. And now he's assigning me the blues.

If I can ever find my iPad in all these boxes, I'll check it out.

"Yep, love you too. Here's Sid."

I handed the phone over. Sid pressed it to his ear with both hands like it was a Poké Ball about to hatch.

"Hi Daddy! Guess what? I caught three Legendaries on the drive!"

Then he ran out of the room with the phone still glued to his cheek.

That's Sid. That's Dad. That's Mom.

And me? Bodhi Dharma. Twelve years old. Stuck in Texas with the blues.

Chapter 2

Dig'n into the Blues

Hot. That was my first thought when I stepped outside the next morning. The kind of hot that sticks to your skin and makes your shirt glue itself to your back.

The old monk said, "Texas shade is just another way of saying thank you."

And the old monk was right. I was thanking every tree I passed on the way to Tire World, pushing my bike with two flat tires.

But I should back up.

The morning started with banging on the front door. The movers. We'd overslept, still stuck on California time. In Oceanside, it would've been two hours earlier, which explained why Sid was still half asleep and why Mom looked like she hadn't had her tea yet. By the time we crawled out of bed, half the morning was already gone.

Eventually, I dug my bike out of a pile in the garage. Both tires were flat, and that's when I remembered I'd loaned my pump to Ollie, back in California. Which made it about as useful to me as a surfboard in Texas. Yes, I have one of those too!

So I walked it down the street to Tire World. Not rode. Walked. In the kind of heat that makes the sidewalk shimmer and your brain feel like it's been microwaved. By the time I finally got there, I was basically begging for air-conditioning.

Once the tires were pumped, I pedaled back, legs heavy, shirt soaked. When I got home, I was sweating like a popsicle in a microwave.

I didn't even bother with sheets. I stretched out on the bare mattress, turned the ceiling fan to high, found my iPad, and decided if I was going to survive Texas, I might as well start with the blues.

I expected the blues to be about guitars and smoky bars. What I didn't expect was a history lesson.

The blues started after the Civil War, when slavery ended. But freedom didn't mean life was easy. Not even close. In the Deep South, a lot of people who had been enslaved didn't own land, so they had to farm other people's fields. At the end of the season, they had to give most of their crops back to the landowner. That system was called sharecropping, and it kept families poor no matter how hard they worked. Days were long, money was short, and the world wasn't fair.

I thought about that, working all year and still ending up with almost nothing. And I complain when my allowance disappears in one trip to the music store.

All that pain had to come out somehow. And the way it came out was music. Not speeches, not essays. Music. Because music could hold the things words alone couldn't.

The blues was about expressing that pain and sharing it. Like, I've got pain. You've got pain. Let's put it into a song and carry it together.

It grew out of the spirituals and work songs people had sung for years, but now it was something more personal. About loss, heartbreak, backbreaking work, and trying to make sense of a hard life.

That's what the blues was, pain turned into music.

The old monk said, "When your heart is too heavy, let the song carry it for you."

And that's what the blues did. It carried things people couldn't carry alone.

I kept reading and found a few songs I could actually look up, the ones that everybody keeps talking about.

"Cross Road Blues" by Robert Johnson. People say it's about a guy standing at a crossroads, not sure where to go, maybe crying out for help. Johnson's guitar wasn't flashy, it was raw, like he was scraping out his soul with every slide and bend. That's the song that fueled the whole myth of him "selling his soul," even though the song's about being lost, not haunted.

Then there's "St. Louis Blues" by Bessie Smith. Written back in 1914 by W.C. Handy, it's about a woman whose heart got broken, made stronger because she says she's as sad as she is mad about what his leaving did to her soul. When she sings, you can feel the room shift.

And "Dust My Broom", another Robert Johnson tune, sounds like a promise to leave bad things behind and not come back. It's got this repeating guitar part that later became one of the most famous blues riffs.

I played them on my iPad, one after the other. The recordings were old and scratchy, but the words and notes sounded huge. I didn't just hear pain, I felt how people wrapped it in music so it wasn't just their burden anymore.

The old monk said, "Every finger line leads to the heart."

And he was right. Each note traveled from my hands straight into my chest. Like the guitar wasn't just wood and strings anymore, it was a bridge. Between my fingers and my heart. Between me and the blues.

Chapter 3
Rock House

Everybody says the most beautiful time of day in Texas is early morning, before the heat cooks your face off. So I set my alarm, grabbed my bike, and hit the road while the sky was still pink.

The air was warm but not frying-pan warm. My tires buzzed on the pavement. Birds argued in the Twin Lakes trees like they were fighting over the last doughnut.

I rolled past the middle school where I'll be stuck in two weeks.

Oceanside had palm trees and open walkways and salt air sneaking through the halls. This place sat low and wide, a brick rectangle with narrow windows that looked shaded even in daylight. You could almost hear the air conditioners humming inside, like the building was already bracing for noon.

A side path slid off behind the houses, smooth concrete curling between trees. A creek moved beside it, slow and brown-green, with dragonflies doing tiny helicopter tricks over the water. Then the trees opened and there was a lake, flat as glass, with two people fishing from a dock and a dog trying very hard to be patient. It smelled like wet dirt and cut grass. Different from home. Not bad. Just different than the Pacific Ocean.

I pedaled on and found it. Rock House. A brick box squeezed between a barber shop with a striped pole and a donut place that smelled like sugar even with the door closed. The windows were tinted so dark I could almost see myself.

The poster on the glass door stopped me in my tracks. It wasn't some computer printout. It looked hand-drawn, the kind of thing you'd see on an old record cover from the '60s. Thick letters bent and curved like they were dancing. Bright colors swirled together, reds, yellows, blues, making waves that pulled your eyes toward the middle. Sunbursts shot across the top, and flowers tangled around the border like they were growing out of the paper.

In the center, bold letters announced: Season Showcase.

At the bottom, someone had written *We Rocked It!* in silver marker, the loops sliding right into the design like it belonged there all along.

It didn't just look like a poster. It looked like a promise. Whoever made it cared. Whoever played that night cared. This wasn't kids messing around. This was kids who treated music like it mattered.

I circled once, staring, then saved the number and name 'Allison' from the sign into my phone. My stomach flipped in a good way. Garage band back in Oceanside was fun. This looked like the next level.

I pushed off again and the path bent behind a park, dropping me at the rec center. Behind the fence stretched a huge outdoor pool, blue under a big white sky. Diving boards at one end. Lap lanes at the other. The air smelled like sunscreen and chlorine and fries from a snack bar that wasn't even open yet. My little brother would lose his mind here.

By the time I got home, the sun was turning mean. Mom was knee-deep in boxes, hair tied back, tape looped around her wrist like a bracelet. My little brother bounced between rooms in his pajamas, narrating everything he saw.

"This box is kitchen. This box is mystery. This box is danger." He lifted the danger box an inch, dropped it with a thud, and nodded. "Definitely danger."

"I found the rec center," I told Mom. "Outdoor pool."

"Pool?" he said, head popping up like a meerkat. "Pool. Pool. Pool!"

Mom smiled without stopping her hands. "If beds get made and boxes get flattened, I can drop you two at noon."

We made beds. We flattened boxes. We argued about where the spoons should live. Mom said near the dishwasher. I said near the cereal. My brother said near his mouth.

At noon we stood at the gate with towels over our shoulders like we were about to storm a castle. The pool glittered. Lifeguards perched high, squinting at the water like hawks.

"Rules," I told my brother. "No pushing. No splashing strangers. If a lifeguard blows a whistle, pretend you did not hear it and then immediately do whatever they say."

"Got it," he said, and sprinted for the diving board.

His first cannonball exploded so big half the shallow end got soaked. A lifeguard shaded his eyes to check the splash radius. A little kid clapped once like he had just seen a magic trick. My brother surfaced with hair in his eyes and yelled, "Ten out of ten!"

I slid in slower. Warm on top, cool underneath. I pushed off and started counting strokes. Twelve down, twelve back. I could not help thinking about the twelve-bar blues. Same idea. Same pattern. It felt like a secret handshake between water and sound.

Meanwhile my brother ran a water circus. The Sideways Shark. The Spinning Octopus. The Sea Turtle With Questions. Three other kids joined in like backup dancers. Even the lifeguard cracked a smile. Acceptable chaos.

We stayed three hours. The snack bar finally opened and the fries made the whole place smell like victory. A vending machine ate two dollars and gave me one granola bar and a life lesson. My brother made a friend named Noah who judged cannonballs with a serious face and then gave tiny thumbs-ups.

When Mom picked us up we were roasted, tired, and dripping. My brother talked the whole way home about the raft he and Noah were going to build and how they might sail it to Mexico.

Back home, after sandwiches on paper plates, I took a quick shower and tried to scrub the chlorine out of my hair. The house felt less like a maze and more like a place people could actually live.

I decided to just text Allison.

'Hi, my name is Bodhi. We just moved to Twin Lakes. I play guitar, and I know a little bass and keyboards too. Mostly rock, but I've just started learning about the blues. I'd like to check out Rock House.'

I read it once, thought about rewriting it, then hit send before I could chicken out.

A few minutes later, my phone buzzed.

Hi Bodhi! Welcome to Twin Lakes. Why don't you come in this week for an audition? Bring your guitar. We've got some groups forming, and I'd like to see where you'd fit best. Allison.

An audition.

My stomach flipped, but not in the bad way. In the roller-coaster way. The kind that says something real is about to happen.

I looked over at my guitar case leaning against the wall. Saturday wasn't just a door anymore. It was a stage.

Chapter 4

Chicago Blues

The next morning Mom asked if we could help clean up the house and put some things together. So Sid and I did a little of that, which mostly meant I taped up boxes and he turned the empty ones into Pokémon battle arenas.

But I already knew what I wanted to do today. Do a little more research on the blues. And start thinking about what I was going to play for my audition on Saturday.

I don't usually play guitar first thing in the morning. My fingers feel stiff, my brain's still half-asleep, and honestly, I'd rather stay up all night playing. I could do that easy, just keep going until the birds start yelling outside. The problem is, that makes mornings at school almost impossible.

So when I was done helping Mom unpack or setting up stuff for Sid, I stretched out on my bed with my iPad and started digging into the blues again. I wanted to know what came after those first singers Dad told me about. Where the music went next.

That's when I found out about Chicago. Turns out, the blues didn't just stay on dusty porches in the South. People carried it north when they moved, looking for work, looking for something better. And when it hit the city, the music plugged in. Electric guitars. Amps. Drums that cracked like thunder. It was still the blues, but louder, sharper, ready to fill up clubs packed with people.

I stopped scrolling. Reading about it wasn't enough anymore. I plugged in my headset, leaned back on the pillow, and hit play.

The first notes slid out slow, like the guitar itself was talking. Not fancy. Not fast. Just honest, the kind of sound that makes you lean closer without even meaning to. A bass thumped underneath like a second heartbeat, steady and heavy. Then came the voice, rough, deep, full of gravel and truth. It wasn't pretty, but it was real.

I closed my eyes. Suddenly I wasn't in my room in Twin Lakes. I was somewhere dark and smoky, with glasses clinking and people stomping their feet in time. The guitar bent one note into another until it felt like the sound itself was bending me. It wasn't just in my ears anymore. It was inside me, like the music had found a place to live.

I listened to Muddy Waters sliding his guitar like it was talking. Willie Dixon thumping a bass line that sounded like footsteps chasing you down an alley. Howlin' Wolf growling into the mic like his voice was half-man, half-storm.

This wasn't just history anymore. This was music you could feel in your chest, like it was alive right there in my room.

I set the iPad down and looked at my guitar. Saturday didn't feel so far away anymore.

Chapter 5
Kung Fu Flamingo

Sid and I went to the pool in the afternoon. What else are you going to do when it's 102?

He likes to turn everything into a competition. So I invented this game where Sid and whatever friend he'd latched onto had to do whatever I called out. I stayed in the water, arms crossed like a judge, while they took turns launching themselves off the side.

"Biggest cannonball." They'd both jump, water exploding everywhere, and I'd hold up imaginary scorecards.

"Best belly flop." Smacks echoed across the pool while Sid came up laughing like it didn't hurt.

"Superman." Arms stretched straight ahead like he was flying.

"Pokémon attack." Don't ask me which one, he knows them all, I don't.

It went on like that for an hour. The kids competing, me calling out the challenges, the lifeguards pretending not to notice. By the time the pool closed, we were waterlogged and sunburned.

We dragged home, dripping flip-flops slapping the sidewalk, and collapsed the second we walked in the door.

After dinner, Mom took us to the Kung Fu studio in Twin Lakes.

Mom is from Dong Guan, China. Inland from Hong Kong. We went there a few times to see relatives. I remember food stalls packed shoulder to shoulder, steam rising from noodle pots, and the smell of dumplings drifting down the street. At night, people sat outside on little plastic stools, talking and laughing while kids chased each other between the tables. It felt noisy and alive, like the whole city was breathing at once.

Mom wants us to stay close to our Chinese roots, so she's always immersing us in Chinese culture. Kung Fu is just part of that. Sid and I got our orange belts back in Oceanside. One of the requirements for moving to a town in Texas was that it also had a traditional Kung Fu school.

The Sifu here trained under a master from Hong Kong who grew up with Jackie Chan. From Mom's perspective, we were in exactly the right place.

The Kung Fu studio wasn't big. A small sitting area in the front with a couple of chairs, a shoe rack, and a bulletin board covered in flyers. The training floor was in the back, padded and marked off in squares that looked like giant puzzle pieces. A handful of students were already working out, their kicks and punches making soft thumps against the air.

Sifu came out to meet us. He was calm but sharp at the same time, like every move he made had a reason. Mom spoke to him in Chinese for a bit, her voice faster and lighter than I usually heard it at home. I caught maybe two words. Sid caught more because he watched cartoons in Chinese.

"When do we get to spar?" Sid blurted.

Sifu's eyes crinkled like he was hiding a smile. "You must be at least an orange belt to spar," he said. "First, you must retest for your orange belt, and he looked at me, and you must retest for your Green Belt, so I know that you have mastered the orange best skills and requirements. I want to see that you know all the fundamentals and ALL of your forms."

I swallowed.

So we set up a time to come back next week and test. If we passed, we could keep training from orange belt and spar. If not… well, I didn't want to think about that.

That's when I remembered something the old monk might say, *"Discipline is the bridge between what you know and what you can.*

When we got in the car, Mom said she picked up something interesting while talking to Sifu. They needed volunteers for the upcoming Dragon Boat Festival. "I think I'll give them a call," she said, already planning it out loud. That was Mom, she couldn't walk into a room without finding a way to help.

Sid was bouncing in his seat the whole ride home, already shadowboxing the air. "I'm going to spar next week. I'm going to spar!"

"Not until we (re)qualify as Kun Fu belts", I reminded him.

He didn't care. He was already halfway to imagining himself in a kung fu movie.

Even as he advanced, he still had to demonstrate that he remembered every form from each previous belt. At White Belt, that meant Tiger Guard, Rushing Step Punch, and the Front Kick Sequence. Yellow Belt added complexity with Dragon Tail Block, Leaping Tiger Form, Emerald Crane Fist, and a Short Sword Form, performed without a blade, using precise hand motions to slice the air. Orange Belt raised the bar with Twin Tiger Claws, Rising Sun Elbow, and Whirling Wind Spin Kick, all demanding sharper control and faster footwork. It also introduced a Staff Form, practiced empty-handed, where each arm became the sweep and strike of a long pole cutting through space.

By Green Belt, memory and mastery were tested even more with Hidden Serpent Stance, Crashing Wave Form, Iron Root Low Sweep, and a Paired Sparring Sequence, again performed without weapons, just disciplined movements tracing invisible steel. A Long Spear Form followed, its thrusts and spirals taught with nothing but body lines and breath, every movement imagining the weight of wood and the reach of a blade. Each level didn't just add new forms; it proved whether he could carry the weight of every move that came before.

"Better practice, Sid," I told him. "Sifu won't be impressed if your Tiger Guard looks like a plucked chicken."

He kicked at the back of the passenger seat. "It's not a plucked chicken. It's a flamingo with power."

I grinned. "Yeah, well, even a flamingo needs balance."

Sid tried to balance on one leg in the seat, arms flapping. Mom sighed and told him to sit down before he kicked out the window.

Chapter 6
Blues Guitar

That night I shut the door to my room, leaned my guitar case against the bed, and sat cross-legged on the floor. The house was finally quiet. Mom was downstairs on her laptop, probably writing emails about the Dragon Boat Festival, and Sid had passed out on the couch after turning the living room into a Pokémon battlefield.

It was my turn.

I pulled out my iPad and searched for blues songs. Not just names this time, the real recordings. If I was going to audition, I needed to *hear* it, *feel* it, and maybe even play it.

The first video was Muddy Waters' *Mannish Boy.* That riff was like somebody stomping on the floorboards in time with your heartbeat. Over and over, never in a hurry. The voice came in rough and proud, like the singer didn't care if you thought he was good, he *knew* he was.

I tried playing along. Just the open-string riff, sliding up the neck the way Muddy did. My fingers buzzed on the frets a little, but when I nailed the rhythm, I felt it. Not fancy. Not fast. Just real.

Then I switched to Robert Johnson. *Cross Road Blues.* The recording was scratchy, like it had been dragged through dust, but the guitar cut through clear. His fingers moved so quick it almost didn't make sense, but under it all was that same blues pattern. A call and response, like he was answering himself.

I couldn't keep up, not even close. But I tried. I slowed it down, broke it into pieces, and felt my way through the chords.

After a while, I set the guitar down and just listened. That's when something clicked.

These songs, they weren't museum pieces. They were alive. And I could hear their fingerprints on the music I already loved. Muddy Waters to Led Zeppelin. Robert Johnson to Cream. Howlin' Wolf to The Rolling Stones.

I pulled up *You Shook Me* by Led Zeppelin. The riff was heavier, louder, dripping with electric power, but it was *Muddy's riff.* Same skeleton, just wearing a leather jacket instead of overalls.

I sat back and thought: *What if that's my audition piece? Start with the blues, then push it into the rock it gave birth to.*

I picked up the guitar again. Played the opening to *Mannish Boy.* Slow, steady, raw. Then shifted into Zeppelin's version. Louder. Faster. Bending the strings like they were about to break.

It didn't come easy. My fingers slipped. Notes buzzed. Half the time I lost the beat. I kept starting over, again and again, trying to hold on to the thread between blues and rock without dropping it.

At one point I threw myself back on the bed and stared at the ceiling. Maybe this was too much. Maybe I should just pick something safe, three chords, strum it out, hope nobody noticed. That would be easier. But easier didn't feel right.

I sat up, grabbed the guitar, and tried again. Slow. Careful. *Mannish Boy.* Into *You Shook Me.* I could almost hear the bridge between them if I leaned into it hard enough.

It reminded me of the first time I tried to learn bar chords. My hand cramped up, my thumb slipped, and the strings buzzed like angry bees. I wanted to quit then, but the old monk said, *"Every buzzing string is just a string that hasn't learned your voice yet."* I hated that he was right.

So I kept going.

Ten tries later, my fingers were sore, my shoulders tense, and I had nothing close to perfect. But every once in a while, just for a second, the sound worked. The old blues and the rock I loved weren't fighting each other anymore. They were shaking hands.

That second was enough to keep me trying.

I set the guitar down at last, flexing my fingers, which felt like overcooked noodles. The iPad screen had gone dark, reflecting my sweaty face back at me.

Saturday wasn't going to be easy. But at least now I knew what I was chasing.

Chapter 7
Crunchy Rice

The next couple of days went by fast. Between the pool, helping Mom get the house in order, and practicing for Saturday, there wasn't a lot of time to sit around. We were starting to get settled in Twin Lakes, Texas, like the boxes were finally disappearing and the house was starting to feel less like somebody else's place.

One night Mom took us to a Korean restaurant. I didn't know what half the things on the menu were, but I found this one dish that came in a hot stone bowl. It was just rice, nothing else, but the bottom layer turned crunchy from the heat. Not burned, not ruined, crunchy. And it was so good. I scraped every last bit off the bottom until the bowl was almost shiny.

After dinner we walked across the street to H Mart, the Korean grocery store. Mom bought one of those stone bowls, a heavy granite crock with a lid, so we could try making the rice at home. I carried the bag out of the store and almost dropped it because the thing weighed like ten Poké Ball sets stacked together. Mom laughed and said it was worth it.

At home, she explained how you make it. Just water and rice in the bowl. Leave it on the stove long enough, and the bottom layer crisps up into that perfect crunch. Simple.

I didn't argue. I was already planning to claim the first serving.

That night, though, wasn't about rice. It was about practice.

Practicing the blues was different from just noodling around. Noodling was easy. You pick up the guitar, mess with some chords, maybe play that one riff you know sounds cool, and put it down. Practicing meant sitting there, over and over, making the same mistakes until your fingers figured it out.

I started with my left hand, the one on the fretboard. The riff for *Mannish Boy* looked simple enough, sliding a couple fingers up and down the neck, just a handful of notes. Except my fingers kept buzzing against the frets. Too soft and the note died. Too hard and it sounded like I was strangling the guitar. Dad always said it's about finding the sweet spot. Easy for him. My "sweet spot" sounded more like sour milk.

Then there was my right hand. Timing. Strumming. Picking the strings clean instead of hitting two at once. That part drove me nuts. The blues isn't about playing fast, it's about *feeling it,* and I had to slow down just to keep from tripping over myself.

"Da-da-da... da-da... da." That's how the riff went in my head. Except when I played it, it came out like "da-dadada-da... whoops."

I probably restarted thirty times before I got a version that sounded even halfway decent.

And then there were the words. Muddy Waters growled like a challenge to the whole world.

Do I sing too? The thought made my stomach twist. It's one thing to play guitar in front of people, it's another to sing at them. My voice still cracked sometimes when I got too loud. What if it cracked right in the middle of the audition? Instant humiliation.

I tried anyway. Half-singing, half-mumbling the words while I played. The problem was my brain refused to do both things at once. If I focused on my fingers, I forgot the words. If I remembered the words, my fingers forgot what to do. It was like trying to rub your stomach, pat your head, and ride a bike all at the same time.

So I broke it down. First just guitar. Then just the words. Then, slowly, putting them together.

The Zeppelin part was even harder. When I switched into *You Shook Me,* the riff was heavier, more stretched out. My fingers had to bend the strings to get that crying sound Jimmy Page was famous for. The first time I tried it, nothing bent. The second time, the string bent all right, and snapped back into my fingertip like a rubber band.

"Ow!"

Sid poked his head in. "Are you losing?"

"It's called practicing," I snapped.

He shrugged and wandered off, probably to build another Lego fortress.

I shook out my hand and tried again. Bend, hold, release. Bend, hold, release. My fingertip was already red and sore, but after a while I started to get it. The note bent higher, like it was crying out, and then fell back down. It almost sounded like singing without words.

That's when I realized maybe I didn't have to sing. Maybe the guitar could do it for me. The words were cool, but if I couldn't sing them right, I could let the strings do the talking.

Still, I scribbled the lyrics down in my notebook. Dad always said writing them out helps lock them in your head. So I practiced the lines, speaking them out loud like I was reading from a spelling test. Over and over until the rhythm of the words matched the rhythm of my strumming.

Little by little, it started to work. Not polished. Not ready for a stage. But I could feel the pieces coming together. Blues into rock. Words into music. Practice into something that might actually sound like a song.

My fingers burned, my throat felt scratchy, and my notebook had doodles all over it from when I zoned out between riffs. But I didn't care. For the first time, it felt like I wasn't just practicing scales or copying somebody else's song.

I was building something.

Practice doesn't make perfect. Practice makes calluses. And once the calluses are there, the music sticks in your fingers, even when your brain forgets.

Chapter 8

School Registration Day

Mom called the Twin Lakes Board of Education and said it was time to get us registered for school. So the next morning we got up, got ourselves together, and headed out.

We started with Sid. First grade. Pretty straightforward.

His school wasn't big, just a low brick building with a playground out back and a flagpole out front. The kind of place where everybody probably knows everybody else. Mom wanted to make sure he got a good teacher, so she asked around while we were there. People nodded and smiled and said nice things about the first-grade class, which Mom took as a good sign.

We even met his teacher. She bent down to Sid's level, smiled, and asked him what he liked to do.

"Legos," Sid said right away. "And Pokémon. And sometimes cannonballs."

The teacher laughed and said, "Well, we don't have a diving board, but we do have plenty of Legos and books."

That was it. Sid was sold. He practically skipped through the classroom, touching the desks and peeking at the bookshelves like it was his new clubhouse. Then we walked around the playground, and he claimed the tallest slide as his.

By the time we left, Sid was already asking how many days until school started. He was all in.

After Sid's victory lap around the playground, it was my turn. Middle school.

The building was huge. Oceanside Middle back in California was big, but this place looked like a fortress. Three stories of red brick, hallways stretching out like a maze, and a parking lot full of minivans that all looked exactly the same. Mom had to ask twice where we were supposed to go just to find the front office.

Inside, kids and parents were lined up with forms in their hands, like we were waiting for tickets to a concert. Except instead of a concert, it was... school.

When it was finally my turn, the lady behind the desk slid me a stack of papers and told me I needed to pick my classes. Sounded simple enough. Until I realized most kids had registered back in the spring. Which meant the "good" electives were already gone.

I still got stuck with the basics: history, algebra, biology, English. Nothing unusual there. But when I got to the elective list, it was like looking at the leftovers after a pizza party.

Band? Full. Art? Full. Theater? Full. Robotics? Full.

The only spots left? "Pioneering" and "Gardening."

I stared at the paper. "What's pioneering?" I whispered to Mom.

She leaned in. "I think it's like camping. Learning how to tie knots and cook over a fire."

Great. Because nothing screams rock and roll like roasting hot dogs on a stick.

And gardening. Digging holes and planting tomatoes. Awesome.

I circled them anyway, because what else was I supposed to do?

By the time we got home, Sid was still buzzing about his playground, and I was wondering how I'd gone from dreaming about guitars and amps to signing up for pioneering and gardening.

At least dinner made up for it. Mom tested out the stone crock she'd bought at H Mart. Just water and rice, cooked until the bottom turned crunchy. When she set the pot on the table, steam curled out, and the smell was amazing. I dug out the crunchy bits from the bottom, and yeah, still my favorite part.

After dinner, Sid crashed in front of the TV, and Mom got back on her laptop. That left me free to grab my guitar.

Saturday was coming fast, and I needed to nail this audition. I started with the blues riff, slow and steady, then tried shifting into Zeppelin. Over and over, starting, stopping, starting again. My fingertips stung, but every once in a while, the notes lined up, and it almost felt like the two songs belonged together.

That second was enough to keep me playing until my hands gave out.

CHAPTER 9

Audition Day

Saturday. Audition day.

I woke up early and hopped on my bike. Just a short ride to get my head together, feel the air, and shake out the nerves. The sun was already heating things up, but it still felt good to be moving. My legs pushed, the wheels spun, and for a little while it was just me, the road, and the sound of tires humming over the pavement.

By the time I got home, sweat was dripping down my back, but my brain felt clearer. That was the point.

We had a late breakfast, eggs, toast, and fruit. Nothing heavy. Never want to eat too much before a show. That's one of Dad's rules. He always says a big meal steals your energy. Your body works on digesting instead of letting your head and your fingers do their thing. Eat too much and you can't think, can't play.

So I kept it light. Enough to feel steady, not stuffed.

Then I headed to my room to tune up, run through the riffs, and wait for the clock to crawl its way toward my audition time.

Mom dropped me off at Rock House, and I finally got to meet Allison in person.

I already knew her from YouTube. She had this Stevie Nicks sort of vibe, so it didn't surprise me when I saw her. I'd seen her cover of "*Rhiannon*" by Fleetwood Mac, and she nailed it. She even looked like Stevie and dressed sort of Stevie Nicks, rock cool.

I told her that when we met. "I saw your *Rihanna* video. That was… amazing."

She smiled like she'd heard it before, but still said, "Thanks, Bodhi. Glad you're here."

Then came paperwork. Always paperwork. Name, grade, instrument. I wrote down "guitar" and tried not to make my handwriting look like I was six.

When that was done, Allison led me back to a room where Jeff, the music director, was waiting. He has the tall Rock look with long hair pulled into a ponytail and a band tee so faded you could barely read it. He nodded at me and pointed to a chair.

"So, Bodhi," he said, "let's see what you got."

My stomach twisted, but I sat down and pulled my guitar from the case. First thing: tuning. Always tuning. You can't walk into an audition and start out flat. I twisted the pegs, plucked each string, listened close. The low E buzzed weird, so I gave it a few more turns until it hummed right.

Allison and Jeff waited, not rushing me. That helped.

When I was ready, I looked up. "Okay… I'm going to start with some blues, then shift into Zeppelin. I want to show how one leads into the other."

Jeff raised an eyebrow. Allison leaned forward. "Cool," she said. "Go for it."

I took a breath. My hands felt sweaty, and for a second I thought I might drop the pick. But then I started.

The opening riff was from *Mannish Boy*. Slow. Heavy. That sliding pattern, up and down the neck, each note sharp like it had something to say. I kept it steady, letting the rhythm carry itself. My foot tapped without me even thinking about it, and for a moment, the nerves disappeared.

I added a little shuffle beat, tried to give it that swing I'd heard in the recordings. Not perfect, but enough to feel like the song was alive.

Then, without stopping, I shifted.

I bent the strings, eased into the opening of *You Shook Me*, Zeppelin's take on the same blues roots. My fingers pressed hard, pulling the strings up just enough to make them cry, then sliding back down. It wasn't smooth like Jimmy Page, not yet, but it was close enough that I could feel the connection.

For three minutes, I lost myself in it. Riff after riff, letting the guitar do the talking. I half-sang a line or two, nothing fancy, just enough to keep the flow. My voice cracked once, but I kept going.

I thought about Dad, about him telling me the blues is where it all started. I thought about Robert Johnson, B.B. King, Muddy Waters. And then I thought about me, this kid in Texas, in a room with two people I barely knew, trying to prove I belonged.

When I hit the last note, I let it ring out, buzzing through the amp until it faded on its own.

Silence for a beat. Just my heart pounding.

Then Allison smiled. "Nice."

Jeff nodded, leaning back in his chair. "You've been listening to the right stuff. Good tone. We can work with that."

I exhaled so hard I almost laughed. Three minutes had felt like three hours.

Chapter 10
Dubai

Sunday morning, the phone buzzed, and Mom handed it to me. "It's your dad."

I pressed it to my ear. "Hi, Dad. How are you?"

Pause.

"Dubai? Seriously? That's cool. How'd you even get there?"

Another pause.

"Oh, right. Airplanes. Duh." I grinned. "What's it like?"

I listened for a second, then laughed. "Hot? Yeah, well, not as hot as Texas. At least you have air-conditioned malls the size of football fields. Here it's just sun, more sun, and… Twin Lakes trees."

I sprawled out on the couch, staring at the ceiling fan spinning above me. "Yeah, we had a good first week. Mostly unpacking boxes. The house is fine. Sid and I went to the pool, ran around, that kind of thing. We also registered for school."

I waited while he asked.

"Sid's thrilled. His first-grade class is small, just one teacher, and he's already claimed the tallest slide on the playground as his. He won't shut up about it."

I hesitated, then added, "Me? I got the basics, but the electives were picked clean. Ended up with pioneering and gardening."

I could almost hear him smirk through the phone.

"Yeah, I know. Rock and roll, right? Tie knots and grow tomatoes. Maybe I'll start a band called *The Garden Tools.*"

He chuckled, but then asked the question I knew was coming.

"The audition? Yeah, I did it yesterday."

I sat up straighter, my stomach flipping just remembering it. "It actually went okay. Better than okay, I think. I started with some blues, slow, steady, sliding up the neck, then shifted into Zeppelin. Tried to show the connection. You know, how one grew out of the other. My hands were shaking at first, but then the music sort of… took over. For three minutes, it felt like the guitar was leading me instead of the other way around."

I paused, waiting.

"Allison owns the Rock House. I told her I saw her *Rhianna* cover on YouTube. She laughed. She really rocked Stevie Nicks. And Jeff, the music director, he nodded a lot. Not much of a talker, but the nods seemed good."

He asked what was next.

"I don't know yet. They're going to put me into a band, but I don't know who with or what songs. I'm hoping for Zeppelin, Cream, Stones, maybe Hendrix if I'm lucky. Could just as easily be Green Day, though. Guess I'll find out."

Then came the part I knew was coming. The homework.

"Yeah, yeah, I know. Keep digging into the blues. Don't just stop at Zeppelin. Muddy Waters, Howlin' Wolf, Robert Johnson. I've been listening. I'll keep at it. I want to actually bring something to rehearsal instead of just pretending."

His voice softened on the other end, even through the static.

"Thanks. It your support meant a lot, Dad. Really. I could feel it yesterday, not just notes, but something deeper. Like when I bent a string just right, I felt it all the way in my chest. Like it connected."

He said something back, and I smiled.

"Yeah. I'll keep at it. I promise. Thanks. Love you too."

I handed the phone off to Sid, who immediately launched into telling Dad about Pokémon battles and how his new teacher promised Legos in the classroom.

I leaned back into the couch cushions, guitar riffs still buzzing in my head. Rock House was coming. Dad had given me my next homework. And I couldn't wait to get started.

Chapter 11
The Dive

After an exciting weekend, Sid and I wanted to go to the pool. It was 102 again, so it wasn't even a choice, it was survival.

The place was packed. Kids splashing, moms talking under umbrellas, lifeguards spinning their whistles like they were on patrol. The concrete around the pool was so hot you had to do this half-run, half-hop dance just to get from your towel to the water without frying your feet.

Sid headed straight for his usual routine: running across the lily pads that floated in a line over the water, falling off, climbing back up, and doing it again. Sometimes he mixed it up with cannonballs off the board, but mostly it was lily pads.

I decided to hit the diving board too. In California, everyone learns to dive. Every pool has a board, and half the kids I knew back in Oceanside could do flips and twists. I wasn't Olympic or anything, but I was a decent diver. A clean front dive, a back dive, even a front flip on good days.

That's when I noticed them. A group of kids about my age, four girls and a couple of guys, sitting near the deep end, half watching the pool, half watching each other. I felt their eyes on me as I climbed the ladder.

So I figured maybe I'd push it just a little. Nothing crazy. Just a double front dive.

I probably should have warmed up a bit with something easier. Maybe I was a little tight. I bounced, launched, tucked, and spun. Except I came out too soon. Way too soon. Instead of slicing into the water clean, I pancaked flat on my face.

Now, I don't know if you've ever done a front dive from a board and landed wrong, but I'll tell you, it hurts. Not the kind of hurt where you black out, but the kind where every nerve in your body yells, "Bad idea!" My chest stung, my face burned, and my arms felt like I'd been slapped by a giant rubber band.

I sank into the deep end and just let myself float there for a second. My plan was simple: push off the bottom, pop up cool, maybe shake the water from my hair like it was all part of the act.

Except apparently, I stayed down a little too long.

The lifeguard must have thought I'd knocked myself out, because the next thing I heard, faint and muffled through the water, was the shrill blast of her whistle.

By the time I kicked up, she was already in the pool. Full rescue mode. Strong strokes cutting through the water toward me. She grabbed my arm just as I was about to surface and practically hauled me out like I was a sack of potatoes.

When we broke the surface, the whole pool was staring. Sid, the kids on the lily pads, the four girls at the deep end, the moms under their umbrellas, even the dads pretending to read magazines. Everyone.

"Are you okay?" the lifeguard shouted, dragging me to the side.

"Yeah," I croaked, water streaming down my face. "I'm fine."

But it was too late. The damage was done. Every other lifeguard had sprinted over. People were standing up, craning their necks to see the kid who almost drowned.

Except I hadn't almost drowned. I'd just landed flat on my face.

Instead of looking like the cool kid who could pull off a double dive, I looked like the doofus who needed saving from himself.

That's when then the old Monk reminded me, "Show off, find out"

And just when I thought the embarrassment was over, Sid yelled on the way out, loud enough for everyone in the parking lot to hear:

"Mom! Mom! Bodhi almost drowned and the lifeguard had to give him mouth-to-mouth!"

I groaned and pulled my towel over my head. Worst pool day ever.

Chapter 12

Blues to Rock

The day after the dive disaster, things finally started looking up.

Allison called.

"Hey, Bodhi," she said. "Rock House's glad to have you. We were impressed with what you did at the audition. So much that we've already signed you up."

I sat up straighter on my bed. "Wait, already? How does that work?"

She explained it. Each semester, Rock House has a theme. One semester might be all Queen, kids learning the songs, studying how Freddie Mercury worked a stage. Another might be Led Zeppelin, or The Rolling Stones, or Green Day. By the end of the session, the band performs a showcase.

"This quarter," Allison said, "the focus is *Blues to Rock.* You'll learn how the blues shaped rock and roll, and your group will play songs that show the connection. Rehearsals start Wednesday night. Full band. And Monday nights, you'll have a private guitar session to sharpen up."

For a second, I couldn't talk. A *band.* Not just me in my room. Not Sid pretending a broom was a mic stand. Not my old Oceanside garage crew fighting over who got to hold the amp cord. A real band. With rehearsals. With an actual plan. With music that mattered.

"Wow," I finally said. "Thanks, Allison. That's… amazing."

After we hung up, I flopped back on my bed, staring at the ceiling fan.

Wednesday night. Full band. Monday night, private lessons. A semester focused on *Blues to Rock.*

This wasn't just a new town anymore. For the first time since we left California, I felt like I wasn't just catching up. I was plugged in.

After lunch, we went to the Twin Lakes Library and got our official Twin Lakes library card.

Sid made a beeline for the kids' section and stacked up a pile almost taller than he was. *Dog Man* by Dav Pilkey. *Captain Underpants,* also by Dav Pilkey. *My Weird*

School by Dan Gutman. And a giant hardback of *The World's Worst Children* by David Walliams, with cartoon kids doing terrible, hilarious things on every page.

For a first grader, he's a serious reader. He'll probably crush it in Twin Lakes Elementary, no problem.

Me? I headed for the music section. I figured if Dad was going to keep piling on blues homework, I might as well come prepared. I picked up *Delta Blues: The Life and Times of the Mississippi Masters Who Revolutionized American Music* by Ted Gioia. Heavy title, but it looked solid. Then I grabbed *Blues Journey* by Walter Dean Myers, it had cool illustrations and poems mixed with history, which felt easier to dive into. For rock, they had *Rock and Roll: An American History* by Paul Friedlander, so I added that too.

Walking out with those books under my arm felt like carrying a stack of secrets. Not math secrets or science facts, but the kind that told you where music came from, who built it, and why it mattered.

For dinner, Mom had her new friend over, a woman who helped organize the Dragon Boat Festival. The house still smelled like cardboard from unpacked boxes, but somehow Mom managed to whip up a spread of stir-fried noodles, steamed dumplings, and bok choy with garlic.

Sid and I shoveled it in, then retreated to the couch with our new library books. He dove straight into *Dog Man*, giggling every two minutes and reading the sound effects out loud, "KAPOW!" "SNORT!", until I told him to cut it out. I stretched out with *Blues Journey* and flipped through the pages of poems and bold paintings of guitars, trains, and singers bent over microphones.

Meanwhile, Mom and her friend sat at the kitchen table, talking in fast, rolling Chinese. Sid and I caught words here and there, *long* (dragon), *chuan* (boat), *yinyue* (music).. Enough to piece together that the Dragon Boat Festival wasn't just about racing sleek boats across the lake. It was food stalls, music stages, drums pounding, bright flags snapping in the wind.

It sounded… cool. Loud. Alive.

Mom was nodding along, already planning. She mentioned setting up a booth for Aumé-Buddhism, with information, maybe some simple meditation demonstrations. Her friend smiled and said it would fit perfectly, the festival was about harmony and community, after all.

I closed my book and thought about it. Dragon boats on the water. Music from the stage. Maybe even a crowd. For the first time since we'd moved, Twin Lakes didn't feel so small.

That night, after Sid finally fell asleep surrounded by his pile of books, I lay awake thinking about two things: dragon boats slicing across the lake… and me, standing on stage with a guitar, trying to keep up with a band.

Old Monk, "Every dragon boat needs rhythm. So does every band."

I wasn't sure yet if I had either. But I was ready to find out.

Chapter 13
Gear it up

I decided to suck it up and go back to the pool with Sid.

Partly because it was hot. Partly because Sid begged. But mostly because the memory of my face-flop disaster kept gnawing at me. I couldn't let that be my first impression at the Twin Lakes pool.

After lunch we packed towels and sunscreen and biked over. The place looked about the same as last time. Same cluster of kids around the diving boards. Same lifeguard twirling her whistle like she was bored but waiting for trouble.

And yeah, they saw me walk in. A couple smiles. A couple comments I couldn't hear. But I knew. They remembered.

Sid didn't care. He shot straight to the waterslide and started doing laps: climb, slide, splash, repeat. I sat in my chair for a minute, watching the board. My chest was tight.

My brain kept replaying that smack of water in my face. But I stood up anyway, walked across the hot concrete, and joined the short line.

By the time it was my turn, the chatter around the pool had quieted. I knew eyes were on me.

In California, diving was almost second nature. Every pool had a board. Every kid learned. It wasn't about being flashy, it was about control. Form. Not making a splash.

I bounced once, twice, then launched. Straight legs, pointed toes, arms slicing the air. I hit clean, slipped into the water like I belonged there.

When I climbed out, people clapped. Not loud, but enough to make my face heat up worse than the sun.

I could've stopped there. Safe. Redeemed.

But no. My brain whispered, *Gear it up.*

So the next dive, I tried a forward somersault. Tight tuck, knees in, and somehow I stuck the landing. More claps. A couple kids gave a quick cheer.

Third dive, I went bigger: a backflip. The world spun, the board blurred past, and for a heartbeat I thought I'd over-rotated. But my feet sliced in just right.

When I came up, a kid at the side grinned. "Nice one."

I grinned back, shook the water out of my hair, and decided that was enough for today. No need to tempt fate.

Later, drying off, I worked up the nerve to actually talk to them. Turned out they were going into 8th grade too. Same grade as me. Same school. One kid played drums, another bass.

"We'll see you next week, right?" one of them asked.

"Yeah," I said, trying to play it cool while my insides buzzed.

For the first time since moving, it felt like I'd landed a dive, not just off the board, but in Twin Lakes too.

Chapter 14

The Retest

Sifu scheduled our retest for Saturday afternoon.

It wasn't just for us. A dozen students were on the list: white belts hoping for yellow, yellows pushing for orange, oranges aiming for green, and even one purple sash. Parents filled folding chairs along the walls, phones and cameras balanced in their hands. The air smelled of mats and sweat, thick with nerves.

Sid and I put on our old Oceanside uniforms. His belt was orange, mine green. But here in Twin Lakes, it didn't matter what we'd worn before. To belong, we had to prove it all over again.

The judges lined up: Sifu in the center, still and unreadable. Two black belts to his left, arms crossed. To his right, a brown belt and a tall teen in purple, eyes sharp as knives.

Sifu clapped once. "Horse stance."

We bowed. Feet apart. Knees bent. Backs straight. Fists at our sides.

The room went silent except for breathing and the faint creak of the mats. Seconds stretched.

At two minutes, Sifu spoke: "White belts, bow out." A handful of kids straightened gratefully and shuffled back, shaking their legs.

The rest of us stayed rooted. My thighs burned. Sid's face was tight, eyes locked ahead.

Thirty seconds later: "Yellow belts, bow out." They rose, some stumbling, sweat dripping down their foreheads.

It was us now, orange and green.

Sid's legs quivered. His breath came fast. He clenched his fists tighter and dropped his weight lower, stubborn.

At the three-minute mark, Sifu called, "Orange belts, bow out."

Sid hesitated. For half a second I thought he'd break. His knees buckled, but then he set his jaw and forced himself up with the others. He didn't collapse. He didn't quit. He had lasted to the end of orange.

But I was still in.

The next two minutes dragged like hours. My thighs screamed, sweat running into my eyes. Every instinct begged me to stand. But I stayed low, fists shaking, breath ragged. The old monk's words echoed in my skull, "Discipline is the bridge between what you know and what you can."

At last, Sifu's voice cut through: "Green belts, bow out."

I straightened slowly, every muscle quivering, the mat swimming under my feet. Five minutes. Done.

"Forms."

We moved through them in rank order. Sid showed his white and yellow belt basics, sharp and focused, then his orange-level techniques: Twin Tiger Claws, Rising Sun Elbow, Whirling Wind Spin Kick. His legs still wobbled from the stance test, but he fought through. When Sifu called for nunchucks, Sid's grip slipped once, the handles slapping against his arm. He winced, recovered, and carried on, snapping the air clean by the end. The judges nodded, and he bowed with a grin breaking through his serious face.

Then it was my turn.

White. Yellow. Orange. Each set building on the last. Then the green-belt forms: Hidden Serpent Stance, Crashing Wave, Iron Root Sweep. Every stance demanded balance from legs that were already half dead, but I forced myself deeper, sharper.

"Weapons."

First came nunchucks. The chain spun through my fingers. Once, the wood clipped my ribs with a sharp sting, but I gritted my teeth and kept flowing until the rhythm settled smooth.

Then the sword form. Invisible steel, heavy in my hands. I cut, parried, swept, thrust. Each motion deliberate, as though the edge could cut air itself.

Last, the bow staff. My arms swept wide, striking and blocking, the invisible pole whistling through space. My balance wavered on one turn, but I locked in, legs burning, breath fierce.

When I finished, silence pressed heavy.

Sifu finally clapped once. "Line up."

We stood side by side with the other students, sweat dripping, legs trembling.

One by one, Sifu tied new belts around waists. Yellow. Orange. Green. Purple.

When he reached Sid, he pulled the orange sash snug. "Strong spirit," he said. Sid's smile almost split his face in two.

When he reached me, Sifu paused, his eyes steady on mine. Then he retied my green belt firm and said, "Discipline holds you up."

It wasn't just a retest. It was belonging. It was proof.

The old monk whispered in my head, "Belts don't hold up pants. They hold up effort."

And this time, I knew exactly what he meant.

On the ride home, Sid leaned forward from the back seat and announced, "Mom, I was sweating like it was a thunderstorm. Every milla-inch of my uniform was soaked."

He paused, proud of himself, then added, "Even the Old Monk couldn't have come up with something better than that."

We all cracked up, the car filling with laughter that finally shook off the weight of the day.

Sid and I high-fived each other in the back seat, grinning through the sweat. I was proud of him for holding strong, and proud of myself for pushing through. For the first time in a long while, it felt like we'd both earned our place, together

Chapter 15
The Sultan

"Hi, Dad. Where are you?"

"Still in Dubai? Birthday party for a Sultan? That's crazy."

I laughed. "You're kidding, right? Twenty-five thousand of his closest friends for a private concert in a soccer stadium?"

I let that sink in. I mean, who even throws a birthday party like that? My birthday last year was pizza, cake, and four kids crammed in our garage with amps turned up too loud. The Sultan got a rock star, a soccer stadium, and probably fireworks.

Dad started talking about his job, the part most people don't see. Everyone thinks it's just flashing lights and screaming crowds. But he said what's interesting is getting the stage and the sound right in every single venue. He compared it to playing an instrument, if one string's off, the whole song sounds wrong.

And every place is different. Indoors, the sound bounces around walls and ceilings. Outdoors, it disappears into the air unless you set it up just right. He said even a soccer stadium changes depending on whether the seats are full, half-full, or empty. If you don't nail it, the crowd hears mud instead of music.

"Yeah, our week was cool too," I said. "It was actually pretty good. I had this weird dive at the pool on Monday, kind of a wipeout, but then I made up for it Wednesday. Got some claps even."

I shifted the phone. "Oh, big news. Allison called. I'm officially in Rock House. This quarter's focus is Blues to Rock. Band rehearsals on Wednesdays, guitar lesson on Mondays. I even picked up a couple books at the library to help me dig into the history. Figured I should actually know what I'm playing."

I paused, grinning a little. "Oh, and Sid and I tested for orange belt. Passed. That felt good."

I thought he'd like that. Dad's not into kung fu like Mom is, but he respects anything that takes practice and discipline.

"Mom? She's been talking with that Chinese lady who manages the Dragon Boat Festival. They want to set up a booth for Aumé-Buddhism. And guess what? They've got live performances too. I might check into that. Haven't talked it through with Mom yet, but still… could be cool. And the dragon boat races? I definitely want to see those."

"Prince?"

Dad must've said something else, because I found myself scribbling another note in the margin of my notebook. Prince. Not just the guy in purple suits, Dad said if I really wanted to hear how deep the blues ran in his playing, I should go on YouTube and watch the George Harrison tribute. *While My Guitar Gently Weeps.* Prince walks out in the middle, no warning, and just melts the place down with a solo that's part blues, part firestorm.

"Okay, okay," I said. "I'll check it out. If Prince is in on the blues, I guess I need to be too."

Talk to you next week, love you!. Here's Sid."

Chapter 16
The Juvies

Only three days till school started on Wednesday.

So yeah, I spent a day at the pool, but nothing big happened there. Just Sid doing cannonballs and me trying not to get sunburned.

The real thing was Monday night: my first guitar lesson at Rock House.

I hadn't been assigned any songs yet since the band rehearsals wouldn't start until Wednesday. Tonight was just me and Arthur, my teacher.

Arthur looked like every guitar guy you've ever imagined, shaggy hair, a faded band T-shirt, jeans with rips that looked earned, not bought. His fingers were thick with calluses, the kind you don't fake, and he cradled his guitar like it was an old mate he'd been traveling with for decades.

He used to play in a London band called *The Juvies* back in the day. They never made it big, but they played the pubs and clubs hard enough to leave their mark. Now, here he was in Twin Lakes, grinning like he still had smoke from the stage lights in his eyes, equal parts old rocker and patient teacher.

"So," he said after we tuned up. "What kind of music are you into?"

I shrugged, then admitted, "A lot of stuff. Lately, I've been digging into the blues, Muddy Waters, Robert Johnson, Howlin' Wolf. My dad kind of gave me an assignment."

Arthur grinned. "Good dad. That's where it all comes from."

"And rock," I added. "Like Zeppelin, Hendrix, The Stones. That kind of thing."

"Classic. You're starting in the right place."

He asked me to show him what I'd been practicing. My fingers felt a little stiff, but I managed a clean twelve-bar blues in E. Nothing fancy, but steady. Then I slid into a riff I'd been working on, the kind that bends the strings just enough to make it cry.

Arthur nodded along, tapping his foot. "Nice feel. You've got good touch for your age."

That made me sit a little straighter.

For the next hour, we went back and forth. He drilled me on chords, A7, D7, E7, the backbone of blues. Then he leaned in and showed me something I hadn't quite seen this way before: how the pentatonic scale wasn't just notes, it was shapes. Boxes. He called it Box 1, a tight little pattern that sat under my fingers perfectly. Then he slid it up the neck to Box 2, then Box 3. "See? These boxes connect. That's how you move across the whole fretboard without getting lost."

I played through Box 1 slowly, then added a bend at the top. It instantly sounded like something out of a Hendrix song. My eyes went wide. Arthur just smiled. "Yeah. That's the language. Five notes, a couple boxes, endless ways to speak."

We even traded fours, where he'd play a line and I'd have to answer it. Sometimes I nailed it. Sometimes I fumbled. But every time, he smiled like that was part of the game.

By the end, my fingers stung, but in the good way.

"That's a solid first hour," Arthur said, putting his guitar down. "Wednesday's band rehearsal is where the real fun starts. Be ready to listen as much as you play."

I packed up, buzzing all the way home. It wasn't just about getting better at guitar. It was about actually stepping into something bigger, like I was finally on the edge of the music instead of just listening to it.

That night, I didn't even pretend to sleep early. As soon as the house went quiet, I pulled out my guitar and ran the boxes again and again. The notes spilled into the dark, clumsy at first, then smoother. Every time my fingers hit the strings, I could feel the shape of something new starting to take hold.

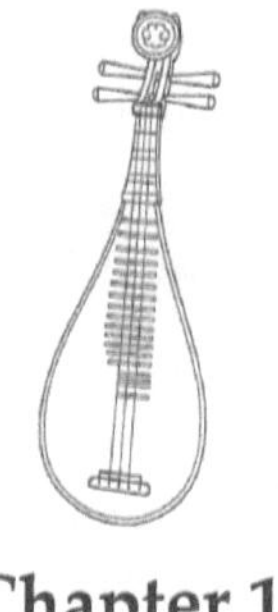

Chapter 17
The Pipa

Tuesday. The last day before back to school.

Sid and I took our bikes out first thing in the morning, before the sun turned everything into an oven. The air still felt heavy, like a warm blanket you couldn't kick off, but at least there was a breeze on the trail. We pedaled past the lake where a couple of people were already fishing, their lines flicking out over the water in slow arcs. Ducks skimmed across the surface, leaving ripples behind them.

Sid kept popping wheelies, shouting, "Did you see that?" every single time. I told him he was going to wipe out and end summer vacation in a cast, but secretly I was impressed.

After a few miles, I asked him what he wanted to do next. He gave me a look like the answer was obvious. "Pool," he said.

So we ended up back at the Twin Lakes pool, our unofficial second home. The water was packed with kids, some goofing off in the shallow end, some racing each other in the lap lanes, and the diving board crowd doing tricks. Sid headed straight for the slide, of course, while I stretched out on a chair with my towel and let the sun beat down.

It was one of those afternoons that felt endless, even though you knew it wasn't. The last lazy day of summer. Tomorrow, the rhythm would change, alarms, homework, teachers, bells. For now, though, it was just water, laughter, and the smell of sunscreen.

I swam a little, dove off the board once or twice, but mostly just floated. Sometimes floating feels like practicing music: you're not moving fast, but you're learning balance, how to stay in rhythm without forcing it.

We stayed until our fingers pruned and Sid was shivering even though the air was still close to a hundred degrees.

At dinner that night, Mom could barely sit still, chopsticks clinking against her bowl as she talked.

"They've confirmed it," she said, her voice bubbling with excitement. "The Dragon Boat Festival will be part of the Fall Festival this October. In China it's called Duanwu Jie. Normally it's in the summer, but here they're blending it with the autumn celebrations. Dragon boats racing across the lake, food stalls, music, lanterns, it will be beautiful."

Her eyes sparkled as she looked at us. "And I'll be running the Aumé-Buddhism booth. They gave me a corner by the water. We'll have tea, incense, maybe some simple meditation demonstrations. I want people to see that Aumé-Buddhism isn't just about books, it's about community and connection."

She leaned forward, painting the picture with her hands.

"When I was a girl in Dongguan, you could hear the festival long before you saw it. The drums were like thunder on the river, guiding the rowers in perfect rhythm. The dragon boats cut through the water, their carved heads painted bright red and gold, teeth bared, eyes fierce. Families lined the banks, shouting encouragement, while smoke from food stalls curled into the summer air. Everyone held bamboo wrapped zongzi, sticky rice dumplings stuffed with beans or pork. It was noisy, messy, alive."

Sid's mouth hung open. "Will they have dumplings here?"

Mom laughed. "Yes. Dumplings, noodles, maybe even mooncakes since it's close to the Mid-Autumn Festival. After the races, we'll all look up at the moon together. In China, that moment means reunion, harmony, being whole."

I leaned back, trying to picture it, the pounding of the drums, the spray of the oars, lanterns glowing at dusk, and

Mom smiling proudly behind her Aumé-Buddhism booth. Twin Lakes didn't feel so small anymore. It felt like something big was coming, and we were part of it.

Then Mom dropped the bomb between bites of bok choy.

"Oh, and good news," she said, way too cheerful. "The Dragon Boat Festival committee has showcase for traditional Chinese talent. Dancing, singing, instruments. They don't allow electronic guitar instruments, but when they asked if you could play the pipa, I told them yes."

I froze, chopsticks halfway to my mouth. "Wait. You what?"

She smiled, proud. "The pipa. It's a traditional instrument, shaped a little like a guitar. Four strings, frets. I thought, well, my son plays guitar, so of course he can play the pipa."

"Mom," I groaned, gripping my hair. "The pipa is not a guitar. It's a completely different instrument. You can't just… swap them!"

She waved me off. "Music is music. You'll figure it out."

"Figure it out?!" I sputtered. "It's like signing me up to fly a plane because I can ride a bike!"

Sid nearly choked on his rice from laughing. "Bodhi's going to play the pipa!" he sang, banging the table like it was a drum. "In front of all the Chinese people in all of Dallas!"

My stomach flipped. "What?! No. No, no, no. Mom, tell me he's exaggerating."

Mom just sipped her tea, smiling like it was already settled.

My stomach flipped. "What?! No. No, no, no. Mom, how many people are even going to be there?"

She set her chopsticks down like it was no big deal. "Last year attendance was about eighteen thousand."

"Eighteen thousand?!" I nearly fell out of my chair. "Mom, that's not a performance. That's a public execution!"

Sid was doubled over, pounding the table. "Pipa Bodhi, live in concert! One night only! No refunds!"

I groaned, sinking lower and lower until my forehead hit the table. "I'm doomed."

I dropped my chopsticks and buried my face in my hands. "Great. Perfect. I'll be the kid who single-handedly embarrasses an entire culture. This is a nightmare."

Sid leaned across the table, grinning ear to ear. "Don't worry. When you mess up, I'll clap the loudest."

"Not helping!" I groaned.

Sid fell over in his chair, giggling. "Pipa Bodhi! Thunder solo!"

"Mom kept eating calmly, like it was all solved. 'A true musician finds the song in any instrument,' she said. Then she smirked. 'That's some Momma Monk for you.'

I slumped back, groaning. "This isn't music. This is a setup."

Sid leaned over and whispered loudly, "Don't break it, or the dragons will come for you."

Mom laughed. I didn't.

Chapter 18
Lion Dance

After dinner, Mom dropped us off at kung fu. The school felt busier than usual, almost like everyone wanted one last hard workout before the school year started. About fifteen kids lined up on the mats. We bowed, stretched, and started running drills. Kicks. Punches. Stances so low my thighs felt like they were on fire.

Then we moved into forms.

Kung fu forms aren't short. They're like dances, complicated, precise, one move flowing into the next. Some of the older students looked incredible, their arms slicing through the air, their legs snapping out in perfect kicks. Watching them made me want to work harder, even when my calves started cramping.

We split into smaller groups. Sid and I worked on our forms with a couple other orange belts, focusing on getting every chamber, every strike, every turn right. Across the room, kids practiced with nunchucks, the wooden handles flashing and clacking together in controlled circles. Another group drilled sword forms, their blades catching the light every time they moved.

At the end, Sifu called us all together. He explained that the school's lion dance team was looking for volunteers.

My ears perked up.

I'd seen lion dancers before in Chinatown back in California, huge, colorful heads bobbing, tails snapping, drums pounding so loud you felt it in your chest. But I'd never been close to it. Never thought I could be part of it.

Sifu said they needed kids to learn the footwork, the rhythm, the teamwork. Some would hold the head, others the tail, and everyone had to move as one. Sid's eyes lit up, but Sifu shook his head gently and told him he'd have to wait until he was bigger. Maybe a year or two.

I didn't even hesitate. "I'll do it," I said.

Sifu smiled and nodded. "Sunday morning. Be there."

I walked out of the studio buzzing. It wasn't just kung fu anymore. It was something louder, brighter, bigger. Something that connected the school to the community.

By the time we got home, the day had finally caught up to me. Sid collapsed on the couch with his Pokémon cards spread out like a general planning battle. I helped Mom fold a few more boxes, then dragged myself upstairs.

We went to bed early that night. tomorrow morning, bright and early, school started.

I lay there in the dark, muscles sore from kung fu, skin still smelling faintly of chlorine, and thought about everything ahead: school, Rock House, kung fu, lion dance. For the first time, I didn't feel like the new kid drifting through someone else's summer.

I felt like maybe, just maybe, I was starting to belong.

Chapter 19

First day of school

The alarm went off at 6:30, and for once I didn't hit snooze. Mom was already in the kitchen making crêpes, sliding them onto a plate like she was running her own breakfast café. Sid stuffed his with strawberries and whipped cream until it was more dessert than breakfast. I just rolled mine up plain and ate it with my fingers. My stomach was already doing nervous flips.

Mom drove us to school, and we joined the line of cars snaking around the block. Horns honked, kids leaned out of back windows waving at friends, and teachers in bright vests tried to keep traffic moving. After ten minutes of inching forward, Mom sighed and pulled into a side street. "We're walking," she said.

The sidewalk buzzed with families heading the same way, kids in new shoes and backpacks almost as big as they were. Sid kept tugging at his straps, adjusting them like he was gearing up for battle.

Inside Twin Lakes Elementary, the hallways were jammed. Kids darted between parents, teachers stood by doors with clipboards, and the smell of crayons and floor wax hit me like a time machine. For Sid's first day, parents were allowed to walk him all the way to his classroom.

We found his room, and there it was: bright posters on the walls, desks lined up in neat rows, a big rug in the corner with the alphabet circling around it. His teacher smiled, introduced herself, and crouched down to Sid's level. He grinned back, already scanning the room like he was picking his favorite spot on the rug.

I leaned against the doorway, watching him hang his backpack on a hook. It felt weird, like I'd blinked and somehow jumped six years forward. I remembered my own first day of school. Sitting at a tiny desk, nervous about whether I'd make friends, wondering if the lunchroom would smell weird. It didn't seem that long ago. And now here I was, walking my little brother into first grade while I was about to start eighth. Crazy.

Mom squeezed Sid's shoulders, kissed his head, and whispered something to him in Chinese. He nodded, serious for half a second before his grin came back. He barely looked up when we left. He was already pulling out Pokémon cards to show the kid next to him.

In the hallway, I glanced at Mom. "He's going to be fine," I said.

She smiled. "So will you."

After we got Sid settled, Mom drove me across town to Twin Lakes Middle. This time there was no walking me in, no holding hands, no classroom tour. She just pulled up to the curb, leaned across the seat, and said, "Good luck, sweetheart. Have a great day."

I nodded, grabbed my backpack, and stepped out before anyone could hear her call me sweetheart.

The front doors loomed a little bigger than I remembered from orientation. I walked inside, and the noise hit me, hundreds of kids shouting, laughing, slamming lockers. It was like stepping into the middle of a band rehearsal where everyone was playing a different song.

The problem was, I didn't actually remember where to go. Sure, we'd walked the halls at orientation, but that had been with a map and a guide. Now it was just me and a piece of paper that said "Period 1: Gardening."

Gardening. My first class in a brand-new school.

I must've looked lost, because a tall guy in khakis and a blue polo stopped near the office doors. He had a walkie-talkie clipped to his belt and a ring of keys jangling. "Need help, son?"

"Uh, yeah," I said, holding out my schedule.

He glanced at it and smiled. "Gardening. You'll like that one. Name's Mr. Robb, assistant principal. Head down this hall, turn left at the trophy case, room 112."

"Thanks," I said, and followed his directions, clutching my schedule like a treasure map.

Room 112 smelled faintly like dirt, even with the door shut. Inside, I saw raised planting boxes pushed against the windows, a few potted herbs on the counter, and posters of vegetables taped up crookedly. At the front stood a woman in her forties with curly brown hair and a wide-brimmed sun hat, indoors.

"I'm Mrs. Thompson," she said brightly, clapping her hands once. "Welcome to Gardening."

I slid into a seat near the back.

The rest of the kids trickled in. Some looked like they belonged there, notebooks already out, eyes scanning the room like they were excited to get their hands dirty. Others looked like me, like they'd just ended up here because all the "good" electives were full. A couple slouched low in their chairs, earbuds hidden in their hoodies.

Mrs. Thompson didn't seem to notice. Or maybe she didn't care. "By the end of this semester," she said, "you'll know how to plant, grow, and harvest your own food. This isn't just a class. It's life skills."

I glanced around at the ragtag mix of faces. Some kids rolled their eyes. Some leaned forward. I wasn't sure which group I belonged in yet.

I figured I'd find out soon enough.

Chapter 20

Gardening

After she took roll, Mrs. Thompson clapped her hands and said, "All right, everyone, follow me."

We shuffled down the hallway, out the back doors, and toward the tennis courts. That's where I saw them: a long row of big wooden boxes, each one full of dirt and tangled weeds that looked like they'd been growing all summer without anyone noticing. Some of the weeds were taller than Sid.

Mrs. Thompson spread her arms like she was unveiling treasure. "This is our classroom," she said. "For the first half of the year, these raised beds will be our focus. You'll learn how to clear them, prepare the soil, check the pH levels, and get the right balance of nutrients. We'll compost, we'll plant, and if we take care of them properly, by December we'll be harvesting cool-season crops. Kale, spinach, lettuce, carrots, radishes. Real food you can actually eat."

A couple kids groaned. One mumbled, "Lettuce? Really?"

Mrs. Thompson ignored them. "In the spring semester, we'll move on to warm-season crops. tomatoes, peppers, beans. But for now, we start with the basics. Soil, water, sun, and you." She pulled a box of gloves, trowels, and trash bags from under the bleachers. "So let's get our hands dirty."

She divided us into groups of four and assigned each group a raised bed. Mine looked like a jungle, weeds sprouting everywhere, dandelions holding the corners like they owned the place.

I pulled on gloves, grabbed a plastic bag, and started yanking weeds while talking to the kid next to me. "Did you know we were actually going to have to do work?" I asked.

He laughed. "What'd you think? We were going to watch videos of farmers?"

I wasn't paying much attention, just grabbing and tossing, when I reached down and pulled at what I thought was another stubborn root. Except it wasn't a root. Or a plant. It was a snake.

A real, live, wriggling snake.

I yelped and dropped it like it was on fire, stumbling backward into the weeds. My arms pinwheeled, my bag of weeds went flying, and I almost sat down in the dirt.

For one frozen second, everyone stared. Then the whole class cracked up.

Mrs. Thompson jogged over and crouched by the snake, which had calmly slithered onto the edge of the bed like this was its territory. "Relax," she said. "It's just a garter snake. Completely harmless."

"That didn't feel harmless!" I said, brushing dirt off my knees while my face turned about three shades of red.

The laughter grew louder, and I felt like crawling into the compost bin. But then the kid next to me nudged my shoulder. "At least you made the first day interesting," he said. That got me to laugh too, even if my heart was still thumping.

Mrs. Thompson used the moment for a lesson. "Snakes like this one are actually helpful in a garden. They eat bugs, slugs, and sometimes even mice. Every creature has a role. Remember that."

The Old Monk said, "Even the snake in the grass is just a gardener with a different uniform."

So my first hour of middle school ended with dirt under my nails, my classmates laughing at me, and a surprise crash course in snake biology. Not exactly how I pictured it, but maybe not the worst start, either.

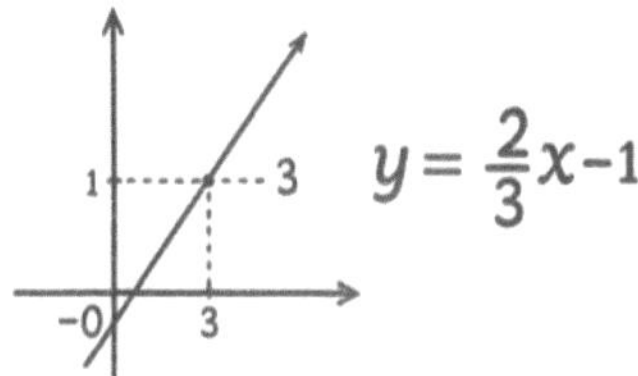

Chapter 21
Algebra

Second class of the day: Algebra.

I'd been nervous, but once the teacher started writing on the board, I realized it was mostly stuff I'd already seen back in pre-algebra. Balancing equations, solving for the mystery number, using letters instead of just numbers.

She wrote on the board:
$2x + 3 = 11$

I didn't even need to think hard. Move the 3 over, divide by 2, x equals 4. Done.

Then she made it trickier:
$3(x, 2) + 5 = 11$

A couple kids groaned. I just worked it out in the margin. Distribute the 3, subtract, divide. Still x equals 4. Funny how different problems kept circling back to the same answer.

By the time we got to graphing simple equations, I was already doodling lines and slopes in the corner of my notebook. Algebra wasn't magic, but it was like a game. Once you learned the rules, the puzzle wasn't scary anymore.

Third class was History. Not just any history. Texas History.

That was brand-new for me.

The teacher, a tall guy with glasses named Mr. Alvarez, passed out a thick syllabus. "This year," he said, "we'll cover the story of Texas. Where it started, how it grew, and why it matters."

He wrote the units on the board:

- Native peoples of Texas
- Spanish exploration and missions
- Independence and the Republic of Texas
- The Alamo
- Statehood and the Civil War
- Oil, cattle, and railroads
- Modern Texas

Some kids nodded like they'd heard it all before. I hadn't. I knew the Alamo was a thing, and I knew Houston was named after some famous guy, but that was about it.

"History isn't about memorizing dates," Mr. Alvarez said. "It's about learning stories. The stories of people who lived before us."

That part stuck with me. Stories. I could get into stories.

After that came lunch.

I pulled out the bento box Mom packed for me: rice and seaweed rolls. When I unwrapped them, I caught a couple kids staring. One whispered, "What is that?"

For a second, I felt like putting the lid back on. But then I noticed I wasn't the only one with a lunch from home. A kid across the table had chickpeas and naan. Another had samosas. A third had dumplings that smelled amazing.

And right across from me was a boy about my age eating rice, too. Plain white rice, neatly packed in a container.

He looked up and gave a small smile. "You… eat rice also?" His English was a little choppy, but I got it.

"Yeah," I said, holding up one of my rolls. "Rice and seaweed. My mom makes it."

He nodded. "Okinawa. My family… move here. My father… Toyota."

That explained the accent. He'd just moved from Japan.

We talked a little, mostly simple stuff, how long he'd been in Twin Lakes (two weeks), how different school was here, how hot Texas felt compared to Okinawa. He didn't say much, but he seemed like a good kid.

And just like that, I had my first friend at Twin Lakes Middle.

The pizza-and-hotdog crowd still looked at me like I was from another planet. But at my table, with kids from India and Japan and me with my seaweed rolls, it felt like maybe I was right where I belonged.

Chapter 22
Pioneering

My first class after lunch was… Pioneering.

When I first saw it on my schedule, I thought it was a typo. Pioneering? Like Little House on the Prairie? I pictured churning butter and wearing bonnets, which didn't exactly scream middle school elective.

But when I walked into the room, I realized I was wrong. Dead wrong.

The classroom smelled faintly of rope and sawdust. Along the walls were shelves stacked with camping stoves, lanterns, coils of rope, and even a stack of life vests. A map of Texas parks covered one bulletin board, and another had pictures of kids in canoes, kids building campfires, and kids hiking with huge backpacks.

The teacher stood at the front, tall with a sun-browned face and short sleeves that showed ropey forearms. He looked more like a scout leader than a middle school teacher. "I'm Mr. Daniels," he said, his voice calm but strong, like he'd spent years teaching people how not to get eaten by bears. "Welcome to Pioneering."

He handed out syllabi, and I skimmed mine quickly. My eyes widened as I read the topics:

- Knot-tying and lashing
- Campfire building and outdoor cooking
- Canoeing and water safety
- Compass reading and basic navigation
- First aid in the wilderness
- Firearm safety and marksmanship
- Archery basics
- Survival shelters
- Team projects: building a bridge and a tower

This wasn't churning butter. This was basically Outdoor Adventure 101.

"By the end of this year," Mr. Daniels said, pacing slowly across the front of the room, "you'll have certifications in boat safety, firearm safety, and basic first aid. You'll know how to build things, fix things, and take care of yourselves in the outdoors. You'll be leaders."

A couple of kids who'd been slouched in their seats sat up straighter. Even I felt a thrill go through me. Certifications. Like actual, official proof that I could do stuff.

Mr. Daniels grabbed a coil of rope from the desk and held it up. "Everything starts with this. The rope. Today, we're going to learn our first two knots, the square knot and the bowline. Every pioneer knows these. One can save your gear, the other can save your life."

He passed out short lengths of rope to each of us.

The square knot came first. Right over left, then left over right. My fingers fumbled a little, but once I got it, it felt satisfying, neat, tight, and easy to remember.

The bowline was trickier. "The rabbit comes out of the hole, around the tree, and back down the hole," Mr. Daniels explained, looping the rope into a small circle. "If you remember the story, you'll remember the knot."

I followed his steps. Loop. Rabbit. Tree. Back down. Pull. A perfect bowline. The rope made a secure little loop that wouldn't slip, no matter how hard I pulled.

"Nice," the kid next to me said, holding up his own messy tangle. "You make it look easy."

I shrugged, grinning. "I play guitar. Guess my fingers are used to twisting around."

That earned a chuckle. For the first time all day, I felt like I wasn't just drifting from class to class. I was actually good at something.

After knots, Mr. Daniels wheeled in a canoe paddle and a life vest. He talked us through boat safety: why you always wear the vest, how to check for loose straps, how to signal with a paddle if you're in trouble. He promised we'd be on the water before the semester ended.

Then he shifted gears again, pulling a bright orange plastic rifle from behind his desk. It wasn't real, it was a training model, but everyone leaned forward anyway.

"Later this semester," he said, "we'll go over firearm safety. No shooting until you've mastered the rules. No exceptions. If you can't repeat the safety steps in your sleep, you don't touch the range. Understood?"

Every kid nodded. Even the ones who'd been whispering in the back suddenly looked serious.

By the end of class, my notebook had more doodles of knots than actual words, and my fingers were sore from tying and untying rope. But I walked out buzzing.

The Old Monk said, 'Any fool can tie a knot, but only the wise know how not to get tangled in it.'

Pioneering wasn't a throwaway elective. It was legit.

On the way to my next class, I thought about how I'd dreaded it when I saw my schedule. Gardening, pioneering, it had felt like the leftovers nobody wanted. But now? Gardening had already given me a snake story, and pioneering might end with me paddling a canoe or shooting a bow and arrow.

Maybe this year was going to surprise me after all.

Chapter 23
English

Last class of the day was English.

Compared to Algebra and Pioneering, it felt almost… normal. Rows of desks. Posters with quotes from writers like Mark Twain and Maya Angelou. A whiteboard at the front with the words *Welcome, Eighth Grade English* written in neat block letters.

The teacher, Mrs. Ramirez, was younger than I expected, maybe late twenties, with dark hair tied back and a stack of books on her desk. She started the period by passing out the syllabus. "This year," she said, "we're going to focus on three things: reading, writing, and critical thinking. We'll be reading novels, practicing essays, and learning how to back up our ideas with evidence. You'll be surprised how much your voice matters when you use it well."

She wrote the year's book list on the board:

- *The Outsiders* by S.E. Hinton
- *Roll of Thunder, Hear My Cry* by Mildred D. Taylor
- *Of Mice and Men* by John Steinbeck
- *To Kill a Mockingbird* by Harper Lee

A couple kids groaned at the idea of that much reading. But I didn't mind. I'd seen the movie version of *The Outsiders* with my dad once, and I was already curious how the book compared.

Mrs. Ramirez assigned the first few chapters of *The Outsiders* for next week and reminded us to keep a reading journal. Then she had us write a one-page reflection: *What does reading mean to you?* I filled the page with stuff about music, how lyrics were like poems, how listening to the blues felt like reading a story in sound. I wasn't sure if it made sense, but it was honest.

The final bell rang, and just like that, my first day at Twin Lakes Middle was over. The hallways exploded with noise as lockers slammed and backpacks thumped. I found my way out front, where Mom was waiting in the car with Sid bouncing in the back seat.

"How was it?" she asked as I climbed in.

"Not bad," I said, which really meant: weird, tiring, but maybe okay.

Sid leaned forward from the back seat, waving his arms. "My teacher read us *Dog Man* and we played outside after lunch and I made two friends who both like Pokémon cards and one of them has Charizard!"

Mom laughed. "Sounds like a good first day."

"It was the best first day ever," Sid declared, sinking back into his seat with a grin.

We went home, and while Sid chattered more about his school, we had some light snacks and fruit. Mom asked me again about my classes, and this time I told her a little more, about the snake in Gardening, about tying knots in Pioneering, about the English teacher assigning *The Outsiders*. She listened, nodding, the way she always does, and smiled.

By five o'clock, Mom was dropping me off again, this time at Rock House.

And that, honestly, was the part of the day I'd been waiting for all along.

Chapter 24
The Band

Mom pulled up to Rock House right on the dot. The building looked even more alive at night than it had the first time, bright glass doors glowing, muffled guitar riffs and drumbeats leaking out every time someone went in or out.

At the front desk sat someone new. "Hi, I'm Mimi," she said, smiling like she'd been waiting for me. "You must be Bodhi."

"That's me," I said, trying to sound more confident than I felt with my guitar case bumping against my leg.

"I'll set you up with a code for the door." She tapped away on the keyboard, then handed me a little card. "Use this every time you check in. Welcome to Rock House."

I swiped in, pushed through the inner door, and followed the sound of music down the hall. A few kids were already hanging out, one leaning against the wall with a bass, another twirling drumsticks like it was second nature, a girl tuning a guitar plastered with stickers. We gave each other the nod. Not a big deal, not a smile, just that quick *I see you, musician-to-musician* thing.

And then Jeff walked in.

He didn't have to introduce himself, you could tell immediately he was the guy in charge. Clipboard under one arm, faded Led Zeppelin T-shirt stretched across his shoulders, and a no-nonsense expression that made the room shift. Everyone straightened, like rehearsal couldn't really start until he showed up.

Jeff ran the show. No doubt about it.

Allison had already warned me: he drove kids hard. High expectations, no excuses. If you flubbed a note, he'd stop the whole band cold and make you play it again. If you came in half-hearted, he'd let you know, loudly. Some kids said he could be tough, even scary. But that's why the music worked.

"Okay, everyone," Jeff said, clapping his hands once. "This quarter, our focus is *Blues to Rock*. We're going back to the roots of rock and roll. That means B.B. King, Muddy Waters, Robert Johnson. From there, we'll jump forward to the bands they inspired, the Stones, Zeppelin, Cream, Hendrix. You'll hear the connection, and you'll play it yourselves. Every show we put on will start with the blues song, then the rock song it influenced. Side by side. The audience will feel it, and so will you."

That got a few nods, even a low "cool" from the bass player.

Jeff scanned the room. His eyes landed on me. "This whole idea came out of a conversation with one of you. Bodhi, right?"

Suddenly everyone was looking at me. My mouth went dry.

"Uh, yeah," I said, shifting my guitar case from one hand to the other. "We just moved here from California. I've been playing guitar for a few years, mostly rock, but I've been digging into the blues lately. My dad's in music, so he kind of… fed me this stuff. I'm really excited to be here and to play with you guys."

Jeff gave a short nod. "Good. Let's do introductions." He pointed at the kid leaning against the wall with the bass.

"Jett," the kid said, brushing his long bangs out of his eyes. "Bass. I've been playing about three years. My dad plays too, so I kind of grew up with it."

The drummer twirled his sticks again. "Colt. Drums. I started on buckets when I was six, got a real kit when I was nine. Pretty much never stopped."

The girl with the sticker-covered guitar raised her hand. "I'm Riley. Guitar and vocals. I mostly sing, but I can hold down rhythm too. My brother plays lead at the high school, so I steal his stuff whenever I can." She smirked, like she'd already been through a dozen bands.

A kid sitting near the keyboards spoke up next. "Name's Max. Keys. I've been playing piano since forever. Classical lessons, but I like messing with rock."

Jeff glanced back at me. "Bodhi, you said you play guitar. You play a little keys too, right?"

"Yeah," I admitted. "Enough to fake it."

"Good," Jeff said. "Max will cover most of the keyboard parts, but I'll throw you some songs on keys too. Riley's got vocals, but you'll sing some as well. We'll switch it up depending on the setlist."

It felt official, like the pieces of a puzzle snapping into place. Bass, drums, guitars, keys, vocals. A real band.

Jeff clapped his hands once, sharp. "All right. That's the lineup. Next rehearsal, we'll put some music in front of you and see if you can handle it. Tonight's just about getting to know each other."

I glanced around the circle of faces, Jett, Colt, Riley, Max. My new bandmates. This was it. My new band.

Chapter 25

Blues and Rock

Jeff clapped his hands once, sharp. "All right, now that we know who's who, let's talk music. This quarter you're not just learning songs, you're learning how rock grew out of the blues. Blues to Rock. That means every blues number we play gets paired with the rock song it inspired."

He turned to the whiteboard and started writing.

"First up: Robert Johnson's *Cross Road Blues*. Without him, you don't get modern guitar. Eric Clapton and Cream turned it into *Crossroads*. You'll play both, raw Delta blues and then full-throttle rock."

Colt twirled his sticks. "So, like, back-to-back?"

"Exactly," Jeff said. "You'll hear how one grew straight out of the other."

He kept writing. "Second pairing: B.B. King's *The Thrill Is Gone,* matched with Led Zeppelin's *Since I've Been Loving You*. Same emotion, different clothes. One aches, the other wails."

My stomach did a flip. Zeppelin. That was right in my lane.

"Third: Muddy Waters' *Hoochie Coochie Man*. That riff is basically the blueprint for rock swagger. The Rolling Stones borrowed that attitude and made *Honky Tonk Women*. That's your pairing."

Jett plucked a low E on his bass, grinning like he was already in the groove.

"And last: Howlin' Wolf's *Smokestack Lightning*. Hypnotic. Gritty. Hendrix carried that same vibe into *Voodoo Child (Slight Return)*. That'll be our closer."

Jeff capped his marker and turned back to us. "That's the setlist. Eight songs, four pairs. By the time you're done, you'll understand exactly where rock came from. And the audience will feel it too."

Riley raised an eyebrow. "That's heavy."

"That's the point," Jeff shot back. "We don't play it safe here. You're going to learn, you're going to sweat, and when you hit the stage, you're going own it."

I looked around at Jett, Colt, Riley, Max. My new bandmates. Zeppelin, Hendrix, Cream, the Stones. This was real.

Jeff checked his watch. "We've got about fifteen minutes left. No sense just standing around. Anybody know any of these songs?"

The room went quiet. I was about to shake my head when Riley raised her hand. "I know a little of *The Thrill Is Gone.* My brother showed me the chords once."

I blinked. That was one of the blues songs. I hadn't pegged Riley for the blues type.

"I've been working on some of the blues too," I added, trying not to sound like I was showing off.

Jeff gave a sharp nod. "Perfect. Let's try it. Riley, you take vocals. Bodhi, guitar. Max, keys, you know the changes?"

Max shrugged, already sliding onto the bench. "I can follow."

"Jett, lay down the bass line. Colt, keep it steady. Nothing fancy yet."

We shuffled into position, plugging in cables, adjusting straps, checking tuners. My hands felt clammy on the fretboard.

Riley strummed a chord, a little tentative. Max dropped in with a soft organ sound. Jett thumped a slow, crawling bass line. Colt tapped his sticks together, one, two, three, four, then slipped into a groove on the snare.

I took a breath and slid into the guitar part. The notes were simple but heavy, bending under my fingers like they carried more weight than usual.

And then Riley sang. Her voice was husky, rough around the edges in a way that fit the song. Not polished, but real.

Something shifted. It didn't sound *good* exactly, but it didn't sound completely awful either. It sounded… like a band trying to find itself.

Jeff stood with his arms crossed, watching, nodding here and there, wincing when we drifted off tempo.

We stumbled through the first verse, scrambled into the chorus, and kind of limped to the end. Jett's bass had gone rogue once, and I'd missed a bend that squealed instead of sang, but when the last note rang out, we all just looked at each other and laughed.

"Not bad," Jeff said finally. "Not good, but not bad. That's a start. You've got the bones of it. Next week, we start putting muscle on those bones. Be ready."

I felt my shoulders relax for the first time all night. We weren't perfect, far from it. But for fifteen minutes, we were a band.

The Old Monk said, 'When strangers play in rhythm, they stop being strangers.'"

Chapter 26

King of the Mountain

Friday night at Twin Lakes Kung Fu was different. That was sparring night.

Sifu always told us it wasn't fighting. It was practice, learning how to move, how to block, how to stay calm when someone was charging right at you.

Sid and I had been waiting for this. Since we passed our retest, it was our first time stepping on the sparring floor here. We carried our heavy bags in, stuffed with headgear, gloves, boots, and cups. The gear smelled like sweat mixed with cleaner, but to us it smelled like belonging.

The only catch? You had to earn sparring by surviving one of the hardest workouts of the week.

We ran laps around the mat, the thin soles of our kung fu shoes slapping in rhythm. Ten laps, then fifteen, then twenty. My lungs burned. My uniform stuck to my back.

Then came stances. Horse stance, low and solid, until my legs felt like jelly. Front stance, back stance, switch on command. "Lower!" Sifu barked, and everyone dropped. My legs shook like crazy, but I forced myself to stay still.

Punches came next. Left, right, left, right. A chorus of fists snapping through the air. Then kicks, front, side, roundhouse, higher, faster, sharper. Sweat ran into my eyes. My hips ached. But I kept going.

Conditioning finished us off. Push-ups on our knuckles. Sit-ups with partners holding our ankles. Burpees that left me gasping. Frog jumps across the mat. Crab walks back. Every muscle complained, but no one dared stop.

By the time Sifu clapped his hands, sweat was dripping down my face and soaking my collar. The younger belts bent over, panting. The older belts stood tall, like this was just another warm-up.

This was the price of sparring night: push yourself to the edge, then gear up.

Gear Up!

Bags hit the floor. Velcro ripped loud as kids strapped on their foot protectors. Gloves thumped as hands slid in and tightened. Helmets bobbled everywhere, cages clicking into place.

The room buzzed with nerves and excitement. A few kids laughed. Others wrestled with stubborn straps. Sid's hands shook as he tried to buckle his gloves, so I tightened them for him and tapped my helmet against his with a grin.

Sifu walked the line, arms folded. "Respect your gear," he said. "It protects you, and it protects your partner."

The sound of shuffling feet, snapping gloves, and helmets clicking shut filled the room like an army suiting up, not to fight, but to learn.

Then Sifu called Sid up.
"Sid versus Chan."

Sid's eyes went wide for a second, then he tugged his gloves tighter and marched onto the mat. He was only six, but he wasn't about to back down. Chan was eight, a solid two years older, with longer arms and legs. Everyone on the sideline knew it would be tough.

The boys bowed, then raised their guards.

"Begin!" Sifu barked.

Sid shot forward first, snapping out a quick front kick. Chan blocked easily and countered with a jab that tapped Sid's helmet. The crowd of kids let out a small "ooooh."

Sid reset, bouncing on his toes the way he'd practiced. He tried a combo, punch, punch, side kick, but Chan's defense was tight. Then Chan came back with a roundhouse that smacked Sid's glove and knocked him a half-step sideways.

Sid growled under his breath and lunged in again, determined. He landed a light strike to Chan's chest pad, and for a second his eyes lit up. But Chan was faster, more polished, and when the match stretched past a minute, it was clear who had control.

"Point, Chan!" Sifu called, ending it.

The two bowed and touched gloves. Chan gave Sid a little grin, not mean, just proud. Sid kept his helmet down, but I could see the frustration burning in his eyes.

Back on the sideline, he yanked at his gloves. "I had him," he muttered, though we both knew Chan's size and experience gave him the edge. He was six, Chan was eight. No surprise in the outcome, but Sid hated losing more than anything.

I leaned in and bumped his shoulder with mine. "You didn't quit. That's what counts."

He didn't answer right away. His jaw clenched, his eyes shiny. Finally he nodded once, sharp, like he was already promising himself the next round would be different.

Sid trudged back to the line, still fuming. Before he could even pull off his gloves, Sifu called up the next challenger, a ten-year-old green belt.

The difference showed right away. The green belt moved smoother, calmer, every step measured. Chan tried the same quick kicks and jabs he'd used on Sid, but this time they didn't land. The older boy blocked, countered, and pressed forward.

Within seconds, Chan was on the defensive. A clean side kick tapped his chest guard. Then another point followed, and Sifu clapped his hands.

"Point. Match."

Chan bowed, breathing hard. This time he was the one walking off with a scowl, while the green belt stood tall in the center, waiting for the next challenger.

hat's when it clicked, we weren't just sparring one by one. It was King of the Mountain. Whoever won stayed. Last one standing would be the champ of the night.

Sifu scanned the line. "Bodhi, up."

My stomach flipped, but I stepped forward. Across from me was Li Wei, a quick, wiry kid with a yellow belt and lightning-fast feet. We bowed, touched gloves, and took our stances.

"Begin!"

Li Wei came at me fast, snapping out a front kick before I'd even settled. I blocked, but the impact rattled up my arm. He was sharp, darting in and out, his strikes landing with speed even if they weren't heavy.

I focused on breathing, remembering Sifu's words, don't chase, hold your ground. I waited for his rhythm, then slid in with a one-two punch and a side kick that tapped his chest guard. The point evened us out, but it didn't make it easier. My legs burned, my arms ached from blocking, and sweat dripped down into my helmet.

Li Wei tried another roundhouse, but this time I slipped it and countered with a clean punch to his midsection pad.

"Point, Bodhi," Sifu called.

We bowed. My chest was heaving, but I had held on. I stayed in the center while Li Wei stepped back to the line, grinning through his mouth guard.

For now, the mountain was mine.

The next three challengers were older than me, but they all wore orange belts. I knew that meant they had experience, but it also meant I had a shot.

The first one, Marcus, came in tall and lanky, throwing long kicks that forced me back. My legs stung from blocking, but I waited for him to overreach. When he did, I stepped inside and landed a quick punch. "Point, Bodhi."

The second was shorter, compact, with a heavy guard. He came at me like a bulldozer, driving me across the mat. My chest burned as I kept retreating, blocking strike after strike. At the last second, I pivoted sideways and slipped a kick under his guard. The room erupted when Sifu called the point.

The third looked the toughest, calm eyes, steady stance, like he wasn't going to make mistakes. We circled for what felt like forever, trading blocked strikes. My arms shook, my breath came in gasps. Finally, I caught him just as he turned his hip for a kick. I shot forward with a punch that tapped his chest protector.

"Point. Match."

Three orange belts in a row. My body was on fire, sweat dripping down my back, but I was still standing in the center.

The mountain was getting harder to hold, but for the moment, it was mine.

Things were about to get serious. The challengers stepping up now weren't just older kids, they were higher belts. First a green, then a purple, and even a brown. Their movements were sharper, their eyes more focused. These weren't just matches anymore; this was climbing into a whole new league.

Chapter 27
The Crown

First up was Sanjit, the green belt. He was fifteen and built like a tank. His punches looked like they could knock a door off its hinges. The trick was simple: don't let him connect. I'd seen him fight before. Slow but heavy. If one of those kicks landed, I'd probably end up stapled to the wall like a poster.

We bowed, and Sifu gave the signal. Sanjit stomped forward, big hands swinging. I pivoted hard to the left, feeling the air move where his fist had just been. I snapped out a roundhouse kick, my foot smacking his chest guard with a satisfying thunk. He reset, came at me again, but every time he swung, I slid out of reach and countered. It felt like playing tag with a bulldozer. Finally, one more pivot-right, one more roundhouse, and the point was mine.

Next was Quin. Oh boy. Quin and I had sparred plenty of times before, and he knew all my best tricks. He was quick, fast on his feet, and sharp enough to cut paper just by looking at it. Sometimes he beat me. Sometimes I beat him. Tonight it was for real.

The whistle blew, and Quin scored first, slipping a jab past my guard. I gritted my teeth, came back with a side kick, and evened it up. One-to-one. Time was running out. I needed something big.

He darted in, expecting the same old combos, but this time I spun. My heel whipped out in a jumping back kick that caught him square in the chest shield. He stumbled back with a surprised look, and Sifu's hand shot up. "Point. Match."

I grinned under my helmet. That one I'd remember.

Then came Kai. The brown belt. Leader of the girls, and honestly, leader of almost everyone. Smart, strong, controlled, she was the kind of fighter who didn't waste a single move. I already knew this was going to be tough.

We bowed. She stood calm, steady as stone. I tried to find an opening, darting left, darting right. I managed to sneak in one point, slipping past her guard with a quick strike. But that just woke her up. The next exchanges were hers, clean, sharp, textbook. She was teaching me while beating me.

I decided to go all in. I rushed forward, hoping to break through before she set her feet. Bad idea.

She spun, and her heel drove into my stomach like a sledgehammer. At the exact same time, my punch was flying forward. Newton's law of motion, right? Equal and opposite forces. Except in this case, all the force went straight into my gut.

The air shot out of me in a whoooof so loud the kids on the sideline gasped. For a second, the world tilted. Then I was on my knees, clutching my chest guard, trying to remember how to breathe.

Kai stepped forward and held out her hand. I took it, still wheezing, and she smiled. "Good fight."

The Old Monk said, "Sometimes wisdom arrives as a spinning kick to the stomach."

We lined up. Sifu's eyes scanned the group.

"Great work today. I want to see more lateral movement, less wasted punches, and better combos. Punches should lead into kicks, and kicks into punches. And remember, when you kick, don't drop your arms. You're just inviting a counterstrike."

We bowed, and I thought class was done. But Sifu lifted his hand.

"One last thing," he said. "The Mid-Autumn Festival is coming up. Our studio has a dragon boat. Many of last year's rowers are now off at college, so I'll need strong volunteers."

Sid and I locked eyes and, without even thinking, shot our hands up at the same time.

Sifu's gaze landed on Sid first. His voice was gentle. "Sid, you have to be twelve to row. I'm sorry."

Sid's arm dropped. He tried to play it cool, but I could see the slump in his shoulders.

Then Sifu turned to me. "Bodhi, you're strong. I'll count on you being there."

Sifu faced the class. "All who are participating in the Dragon Boat Races will perform our forms at the event. We will honor our culture and our commitment to Kung Fu.

My lungs were still burning from the fight, but I couldn't help it, my chest swelled a little. It felt good to be trusted, even if I was still trying to suck in air like a fish on land.

Chapter 28

Strings on Fire

Saturday morning was weirdly quiet. Mom had gone off early to some volunteering thing, Sid was on the floor surrounded by Lego bricks (his army of half-built robots staring me down), and I was left sitting there with Dad's "homework" echoing in my head.

So I pulled up YouTube and searched for While My Guitar Gently Weeps. The one Dad told me about, the George Harrison tribute with Prince, Clapton, Tom Petty, all those legends lined up like it was Mount Rushmore for rock.

At first it was mellow. Clapton and the others traded licks, all smooth and respectful, like they were at a fancy dinner and didn't want to spill the soup. Then Prince stepped up.

And man. The dude didn't just play the guitar. He set it on fire without fire. His solo didn't sound like note, it sounded like something alive, wailing, clawing, laughing, all at the same time. He bent one note so long I thought my Wi-Fi froze, then he slid into this crazy run up the neck, faster than I even thought possible. Half the crowd looked like their jaws hit the floor. Clapton was nodding like, "Yeah, okay, the kid's not human."

And the ending? Prince played so hard the guitar looked like it gave up. Then he literally tossed it straight up into the air, walked off like nothing happened, and, poof, the guitar never came back down. I swear it vanished into another dimension.

I had to pause the video just to breathe.

That's when I started wondering. What made Prince… well, Prince? So I dug into his background.

Turns out, he grew up in Minneapolis with music basically dripping from the walls. His dad was a jazz pianist, his mom was a singer, and little Prince was surrounded by instruments before he could probably spell "instrument." He didn't just pick one, he taught himself all of them. Guitar, bass, keys, drums, the works. Like, who does that? By the time I was his age, I was still trying to tie my shoelaces tight enough so they didn't flap when I ran.

But the coolest thing I found? Prince was built on the blues. He didn't always advertise it, but it was always in there. You could hear it when he bent a string until it cried, or when he let a note hang just long enough to make your chest ache.

What made him different was how he used the blues. Most players stay in their lane, rock guys, blues guys, funk guys. Prince basically said, "Nah." He mixed everything. Funk, soul, jazz, gospel, rock, pop, he just smashed it all together and somehow made it sound perfect. He wasn't just breaking rules, he was living like the rules never existed.

Watching that solo again, it hit me. Prince wasn't just showing off. He was saying the blues wasn't stuck in the past. It could wear purple heels, dance across a stadium stage, and still knock the air out of your lungs.

I leaned back, headphones buzzing in my ears, and grinned. Maybe Dad was right. The point isn't to play the blues exactly like Muddy Waters or B.B. King. It's to take it, bend it, twist it, and make it mine. Kind of like Prince did. Just… maybe without the ruffled shirt.

And for once, practicing scales didn't feel like punishment. It felt like unlocking a cheat code.

Chapter 29

The Lunch

Mom came home buzzing with energy from her Dragon Boat Festival friends, her arms loaded with bags that smelled way better than anything we had in the fridge. She set them on the counter like treasure. Out came boxes of steamed dumplings, plump and shiny with garlic and chive. Next was a tray of scallion pancakes, golden and crispy around the edges, stacked like floppy records. She had sesame balls dusted with sugar, their centers oozing sweet red bean paste when you bit into them, and a little paper box of mooncakes, each stamped with a delicate design on top like tiny works of art.

The kitchen filled with the warm, savory smell of soy, ginger, and fried dough. Sid darted over first, lifting the lid on everything like he was inspecting presents, his eyes wide at the desserts. I tried to act cool, but my stomach growled so loud it gave me away. It felt like Mom had brought the festival home with her.

"So you like that food? It came from my new friend, Meiling. She made all of it by hand, and she hopes you enjoy it."

"Her father recently passed, and she has been grieving. I've been helping her work through her sorrow. I told her about the Dragon Boat Festival, and she agreed to join me at the Aumé–Buddhism booth for the event."

Somewhere deep down, I already knew something was coming. Bodhi put his hands to the sides of his head, seeing it unfold before him.".

"I also told her you would be performing, and though it was hard for her to let go, she felt her father would want someone who could truly play the pipa to have it. So she has given you her father's pipa.

Mom, I told you before. I don't want to play the pipa at the festival. I really thought you understood?

"Bodhi, you don't understand. She just lost her father, and he loved the pipa. She's giving it to you with love, trusting that you'll treasure it the way he did. At least take a look. You might even find you like it."

"Bodhi, I think it's a sign from Aumé that you should have the Pipa and play it."

Bodhi went out to the car and wrestled the pipa box from the trunk. The case looked ancient, its corners patched up with layers of tape that had gone yellow with age. Back in his room, he set it carefully on the bed. Then he sat down beside it, staring like it might suddenly open on its own. Part of him wanted to rip off the tape and dive in. The other part felt like he was holding a secret too big for him.

He peeled back the last strip of tape and lifted the lid. Inside, resting on a faded silk lining, was the pipa.

It was nothing like the beat-up school guitars Bodhi was used to. The body was shaped like a teardrop, carved from pale wood that had darkened at the edges with age. The finish glowed softly, almost like honey in sunlight. The frets climbed high up the neck in perfect little steps, more than any guitar he'd ever seen.

The strings shimmered, stretched tight across a carved bridge shaped like a tiny dragon. At the top, the tuning pegs fanned out like wings, each one capped with smooth ivory-colored knobs. The whole instrument looked like it had been designed for both music and magic.

Even the smell of it was different. A mix of wood, old varnish, and something sweet he couldn't name. Bodhi leaned closer, almost afraid to touch it.

"This is… whoa," he whispered to nobody. "Not a guitar. Not even close.

"How do you even tune this thing?" Bodhi muttered, twisting the case around like it might give him instructions.

He pulled out his phone and searched: how to tune a pipa. A dozen videos popped up, all with people who looked way too calm for how complicated this seemed.

He tapped one. A woman in flowing robes plucked a note, then another, adjusting the pegs with gentle precision. "Standard tuning is A–D–E–A," she said in a soft voice.

Bodhi frowned. "Wait, what? A–D–E–A? That's not even a real tuning. That's like… a broken video game code."

He balanced the pipa on his lap, awkwardly holding it upright the way the video showed. The instrument felt big and slippery, nothing like his dad's guitars. He turned the first peg slowly. The string creaked higher, then lower, then pinged like a rubber band.

"Okay… okay… easy there," Bodhi said under his breath, as if the pipa could hear him. He plucked again, comparing it to the sound on the video. Too low. Twist, pluck, twist. The note rose, closer this time. He tried the next string, then the next, fingers fumbling with the wide frets.

By the time he got through all four strings, his forehead was sweaty and his stomach was growling. But when he strummed gently across them, the sound rang out, bright, bell-like, and way prettier than he expected.

Bodhi blinked. "Whoa. That's… not terrible. Actually, that's kind of awesome."

"Okay… now what do I play?" Bodhi asked the room. The pipa didn't answer, just gleamed back at him like it was daring him to try.

He plucked one string, then another, hunting for something familiar. The notes didn't line up like a guitar, and the frets were spaced so close together it felt like trying to text with mittens on. He slid his finger up and down, listening to how the pitch jumped from low to high.

After a few minutes of messing around, patterns began to show themselves. He found a little riff, two high plinks followed by a deep, twangy note. It wasn't much, but it reminded him of the way his dad once described Jimmy Page messing with new tunings: "Sometimes you just chase the sound until it surprises you."

He tried forming a chord, pressing down two strings at once. The sound buzzed, rough and uneven, like a bee trapped in a soda can. He laughed. "Okay, so that's not a chord."

But then, by accident, his fingers landed on a shape that rang out clean and rich. Four notes together, shimmering in the air. Bodhi froze. He plucked it again. Then again.

"This is wild," he whispered. "It's like... the guitar's weird cousin. Smarter, older, kind of showing off."

The longer he played, the more the strings seemed to guide him instead of the other way around. Little melodies slipped out, strange but beautiful, like he'd opened a secret door and found music waiting on the other side.

Once he got the hang of the strings, Bodhi thought, Why not? Let's try some blues.

It just seemed right. The pipa wasn't built for Muddy Waters or B.B. King, but as he bent into a slow, dragging riff, it was like the instrument sighed with him. The notes came out brighter and sharper than a guitar, almost like tears shining in the air.

For a moment, Bodhi could almost picture the man who had owned it before, an old father sitting by the window, listening, a little sad, a little proud. It felt like the music reached across time, stitching them together.

Surprisingly, it worked. The pipa could moan, it could swing, it could even cry in that sweet, aching way the blues demanded. Bodhi grinned, shaking his head. "Blues on a pipa. Who would've thought?"

One song bled into another. Riffs he'd picked up from his dad, little licks he half-remembered from old records, even a clumsy version of "Crossroads." The pipa answered each time with its own voice, ancient, sharp, but warm.

Hours passed without him noticing. The glow from his desk lamp made the room feel smaller, almost like a stage.

Then a memory rose in his mind, one of the old monk's sayings he had heard back at the temple: "Every string carries two songs, the one you play, and the one that plays you."

Bodhi let the words settle as he leaned back. The monk was right. Tonight wasn't just about him making music. The pipa had its own story, and somehow, they were telling it together.

Chapter 30
Lion Dance Practice

Bodhi wasn't sure what he was expecting. Maybe some drumming, some costumes, a few goofy moves to make the lion's head nod. He definitely wasn't expecting sweat pouring down his back after ten minutes, or the serious, focused faces of the other kids in the room.

The practice was held at a sister Kung Fu studio across town. The place smelled of wood polish and tiger balm, and the mats squeaked under their bare feet. About a dozen kids had shown up, six girls, all around his age up to maybe sixteen, and about the same number of boys. Almost all of them wore green belts or higher. Bodhi tugged at his plain white sash, suddenly feeling like a cub who had wandered into a pride of lions.

The instructor, Sifu Huang, clapped his hands. "Lion dance is Kung Fu with spirit," he said. "The lion does not just move. It breathes. It listens. It becomes alive. Today, you will learn to give it life."

Bodhi's eyes darted to the huge lion heads stacked against the wall. Each was covered in bright fur, with painted wooden faces that seemed to glare or grin depending on how the light hit them. Their tails, long and flowing, were folded neatly beside.

The first lesson wasn't even with the costume. It was footwork. The group lined up, and Sifu called out stances: horse stance, bow stance, cat stance. Then he added bouncing, shifting weight from one leg to the other, moving forward in a rhythm that felt part march, part dance.

"Again!" Sifu barked, and they repeated it until Bodhi's thighs burned.

Next came the lion's personality. "A lion is curious," Sifu explained, demonstrating with quick, jerky head movements, eyes darting side to side. "Then it becomes playful." He crouched, hopping forward in a way that made the imaginary lion seem almost puppy-like. "Then powerful." He stomped into a bow stance, punching with both fists as if swiping claws.

Finally, the costumes came out. Two people per lion: one in the head, one in the tail. Bodhi got paired with a taller girl named May, who already had a blue sash. She took the head, leaving Bodhi in the tail.

"Don't think of it as just holding the back," May whispered. "You're the lion's spine. If you're weak, the whole thing collapses."

The head was heavy, even though May made it look easy, snapping it up and down to make the eyes blink and the mouth clack. Bodhi hunched low, grabbing the tail and trying to follow her movements. Every step had to match hers. Every bounce, every hop, every shift of weight. When she crouched to make the lion "eat" a lettuce head from the floor, Bodhi had to bend too, nearly losing his balance.

It was harder than any sparring drill he'd ever done. His legs shook, his arms ached, and sweat dripped into his eyes. But when they finally stumbled through a short sequence and the drum thundered at the far end of the room, something clicked. The beat made his chest vibrate, and for a few seconds, it didn't feel like two kids in a costume. It felt like one creature, alive and fierce, moving to the rhythm of the drum.

Afterward, Bodhi collapsed onto the mat, panting. May grinned, handing him a water bottle. "Not bad for your first time, white sash. You've got spirit. That's half the battle."

Bodhi gulped water and managed a crooked smile. "Yeah. Spirit. The other half must be surviving leg day."

The group laughed, and Sifu clapped once more. "Good. You have begun. Remember: in lion dance, you don't just wear the lion. You become the lion. Train hard, and people will forget there are two humans inside. They will only see the lion."

Just when Bodhi thought they were done, Sifu Huang clapped his hands again. "Again! This time with the music."

Two older students took their places at the instruments. One raised heavy wooden drumsticks above the giant war drum, another lifted gleaming brass cymbals, and a third held a gong.

The first beat hit like thunder. BOOM, BOOM, BOOM. The cymbals clashed, the gong growled, and suddenly the whole studio shook with rhythm.

"Head up! Tail strong!" Sifu shouted.

May jerked the lion's head to the beat, blinking the eyes and snapping the jaw. Bodhi bent low in the tail, copying every bounce and turn. The drum drove them forward, faster than before. His thighs screamed, but there was no stopping. When the beat rolled into a fast rhythm, they had to leap, crouch, and twist in perfect sync.

"Make the lion breathe!" Sifu yelled.

May lifted the head high, then dipped low, making the lion look curious, then fierce. Bodhi followed, sweat flying off his face as he tried to keep the tail from lagging. The cymbals clashed in wild bursts, and the gong rang out as the lion "attacked" the invisible enemy in the air.

By the end, Bodhi's legs were jelly and his arms shook like noodles, but when the drum gave its final crash and they froze in a bow stance, he felt something spark inside him. The lion costume was heavy, the movements exhausting, but for a few moments it felt like they weren't just kids pretending. They were the lion, proud, fierce, alive.

May flipped the head back, grinning at him through her damp hair. "Told you the tail matters."

Bodhi could only nod, trying to catch his breath. "Next time," he puffed, "I'm calling dibs on the head."

The whole class laughed, and the drum rumbled again like it was in on the joke.

Before Bodhi knew it, practice was over. His shirt clung to him, his hair was plastered to his forehead, and his legs felt like wobbly Jell-O.

"Line up!" Sifu Huang's voice snapped through the air like a drumbeat. Everyone scrambled into rows, panting but standing tall.

Sifu paced in front of them, hands behind his back. "Good job today. You worked hard. But this is just the beginning. We lost a number of our senior performers to college, which means this year the lion depends on you." His gaze swept across the line, resting on each face, sharp but proud.

"I need commitment. Do I have it?"

"Yes, Sifu!" the group shouted in unison. Bodhi's voice cracked halfway, but he shouted anyway.

Sifu's eyes softened just a little. "Good. We have only four more weeks until the Dragon Boat Festival. Four weeks to master your roles and represent our Kung Fu family, and Chinese culture, at its best. Train hard, trust each other, and remember… a lion without spirit is just cloth and wood. But a lion with spirit can move mountains."

The cymbals clashed once, as if on cue, and the group bowed together.

It was the cymbals that did it.

The crash echoed in his head long after the sound had faded. A crash like thunder. A crash like the world shutting a door he couldn't open again.

Bodhi's grin froze. His stomach dropped.

Oh no.

Somehow, without realizing it, he had just committed to… everything.

The Dragon Boat Festival wasn't just some weekend party with dumplings and lanterns. It was the event, the biggest celebration of the year. And now, Bodhi was locked into rowing in the Dragon Boat races with his Kung Fu school team, performing his Kung Fu forms with the other students, carrying the tail of a lion in the Lion Dance troupe, and, oh yeah, playing the pipa on stage in front of eighteen thousand people.

Eighteen. Thousand. People.

His chest tightened. Sweat that had nothing to do with practice prickled at the back of his neck.

What was he thinking?

Bodhi glanced down the line at the other kids. May, still holding the lion's head, was standing tall and proud. The others looked serious too, but also… ready. Committed. Like they belonged here.

And him? He felt like he had just strapped himself to a rocket that was already blasting off.

The cymbal crash echoed again in his brain, louder this time, rattling around like a giant warning bell.

What if I let everyone down? What if I mess up the rowing rhythm and our boat sinks? What if I trip in the middle of the Lion Dance and the whole lion falls apart? What if I freeze with the pipa in my hands and eighteen thousand people stare at me in silence?

The more he thought about it, the more impossible it seemed. It was too much. Too big. Too many promises.

And the worst part? They weren't just promises to himself. They were promises to people. To his new friends at Kung Fu school. To May, who trusted him to be the spine of the lion. To Sifu, who believed in him even though he was only a white sash. To his mom, who had asked him to honor the pipa. To his dad, who always told him that music was about courage.

Bodhi's heart thumped so hard he thought the drum might pick it up and pound it louder.

What was he going to do?

For the first time since moving to Twin Lakes, Bodhi felt the full weight of it all, the culture, the expectations, the friendships, the music, the Festival. Everything was pulling at him at once, and the cymbal crash wouldn't stop ringing.

Chapter 31
Indian Wedding

"Hi, Dad. How are you?"

"Great, all good to hear."

"So… where are you now?"

"Mumbai? Wait. Did you just say… an Indian wedding in Mumbai? Like, an actual wedding? And the star is performing there? That's insane. How can someone even afford that?"

"Hold on, hold on. Did you say fifty million dollars? For a wedding?"

"And, wait a second, twenty-five thousand people? And the cost is… what? One hundred million? The entire wedding cost one hundred million dollars? You're not joking?"

"Wait, wait, do they have elephants? Please tell me there are elephants. Or, like, a fountain of soda? A cake so big it has its own zip code? Because if you're spending a hundred million dollars, you can't just hand out regular wedding cake and call it a day."

Okay, stop. Let me just picture this for a second. Twenty-five thousand guests. That's like if you took our entire town of Twin Lakes and stuffed everybody into one giant ballroom with cake. Not just a sheet cake either, more like a cake taller than the water tower, with stairs and an elevator. Maybe elephants carrying slices to the back row. Golden microphones for the speeches. Fireworks every five minutes so nobody nods off.

Back to Dad. "Wow. Just... wow."

"So how's it going for you? Cool? Big stage? Bright lights?"
"Nice."

Meanwhile, my life feels tiny in comparison. But still,
"Yeah, I'm doing pretty good here too. Making friends. And Rock School is awesome. You'll like this: my band is playing something called Blues to Rock. We've got four sets. Each starts with a blues song, then we play the rock song it inspired. Like musical dominoes. Pretty cool, right?"

I mean, come on. Robert Johnson's Cross Road Blues sliding right into Cream's Crossroads. That's like tasting the recipe and then biting the final dish. Even my math teacher was tapping her pencil to the beat. Math teachers don't tap pencils unless they're secretly enjoying themselves.

"Hey, um, I need your advice on something. The Mid-Autumn Festival's coming up here, and Twin Lakes is doing this huge Dragon Boat Race."

"Yeah, it's pretty cool."

"But here's the thing, I kind of… overcommitted myself."

"At the Dragon Boat, Mid-Autumn Festival, I am on the rowing team. And I'm performing Kung Fu forms. And I somehow agreed to do a lion dance in the parade. And, this is the kicker, Mom committed me to playing the pipa in front of eighteen thousand people!"

"Yeah, Dad, you heard me right. Eighteen. Thousand. People. I thought maybe she meant eighteen, like a couple rows of folding chairs. Nope. Try eighteen thousand."

"Dad… are you okay? Ha ha, very funny. It's not that funny! What should I do?"

Of course he says: "Just make it happen." That's classic Dad.

Sure, Dad is used to juggling a lot of things, last-minute venue changes, sound systems that go haywire, and apparently weddings and birthdays for the super-rich. But this is all new to me.

The old monk said, "You cannot row the whole river in one stroke."

"Easier said than done. But... okay, okay. Break it into chunks, do one thing at a time. Got it. The roadie way of life."

Wish me luck. Seriously. Because right now, my life feels like a twelve-layer wedding cake, and I'm supposed to eat the whole thing with one fork.

"Alright, here's Sid. Love you, Dad. Bye."

Chapter 32

Lunch with Riley

After we dropped off Sid at elementary school, Mom dropped me at Twin Lakes Middle. Gardening first period was the usual, dirt under my fingernails and a teacher who talks to tomato plants like they're royalty.

By lunch, I was starving. I found a spot at an empty table, set down my tray, and opened the bento Mom had packed: rice with seaweed, some pickled radish, and slices of apple. The cafeteria smelled like french fries and mystery pizza, but honestly, I'd take Mom's rice and seaweed any day.

I had just gotten my chopsticks out when Riley slid onto the bench next to me, plunking her juice box down like it was a drumstick.

"Hi, rock boy," she said. "I like the shirt."

I looked down at my Doors T-shirt. "Thanks. I like yours too. Cool?"

She was wearing a Cure shirt, black with faded letters. "So are we the only two rockers at this school?" she asked. "You with The Doors, me with The Cure. Totally different decades, but still."

I grinned. "Guess we're a two-person revolution."

"More like two weirdos," she said, laughing.

"You mind if I sit here?"

"No, awesome. Good to see you." I hesitated, then added, "Honestly, I thought you were in high school."

She nearly spit out her juice. "No, dummy. You're older than me. I'm in seventh grade."

I almost dropped my chopsticks. "Wait, seriously? Seventh grade? But at Rock School you were so confident I thought you had to be older."

She shrugged. "Guess confidence adds a couple years."

We laughed, then I asked, "So how was your weekend?"

Riley groaned. "Don't ask. My older brother Jack totally monopolized everything. He picked the movie, hogged the

Xbox, and even called dibs on the last slice of pizza. Basically, the Jack Show, starring Jack."

I snorted. "I'm sure Sid would say the same thing about me. Big brothers are professional monopolizers."

"Yeah, but Jack's practically an Olympic champion at it," she said, stabbing her straw into her juice box.

I poked at my rice. "Well, if it makes you feel better, I'm about to drown this week. The Dragon Boat–Mid-Autumn Festival is coming up, and I kind of signed myself up for… everything."

Her eyes lit up. "Dragon Boat–Mid-Autumn Festival? What's that?"

"Okay, picture this," I said, setting my chopsticks down.

"There's a huge lake, and on the lake are these long, skinny boats painted like dragons. Each one has a team of rowers paddling in sync, and a drummer at the front keeping the beat. It's like a race, but also like a parade on water. Around the lake, there are booths with food and games. Mom even has an Aumé-Buddhism booth. And the whole thing goes all day, with music and performances, until they close it around six."

Riley's eyebrows shot up. "Whoa. That sounds amazing."

I leaned closer. "It's also exhausting. I'm rowing in the dragon boat, performing Kung Fu forms, doing a lion dance in the parade, and, just to top it off, playing the pipa in front of eighteen thousand people."

She dropped her chip. "Eighteen thousand?!"

"Okay, maybe not all at once," I admitted. "The festival has about eighteen thousand people. Maybe only twelve thousand will actually watch me play. But still, that's a lot of eyeballs staring at me."

She tilted her head. "Wait. I didn't even know you had a pipa. Or played a pipa. Or… okay, what is a pipa?"

I picked up my chopsticks again and held them like an instrument. "It's a Chinese instrument. Kind of like a lute."

Riley squinted. "What's a lute?"

"Uh… think old-timey guitar. Like the grandparent of the guitar."

Her face lit up. "Ohhh, so the pipa is like a cousin of the guitar?"

"Exactly!" I said. "But instead of strumming chords, you pluck really fast with your fingers. Sometimes it sounds like raindrops, sometimes like galloping horses, sometimes both at the same time."

Riley's eyes went wide. "So you're basically saying you're going to rock out on a Chinese guitar in front of twelve thousand people?"

"Yep," I said with a grin. "Except I can't smash it on stage. I have to hand it back to Mom."

She laughed so hard her juice almost came out her nose. "I have to see this. Mind if I come?"

I blinked, then nodded. "That would be great!"

And just like that, my stress about the Dragon Boat, Mid Autumn Festival felt a little lighter. Still a lot. But lighter

Chapter 33

Guitar Lesson

Monday evening I had my lesson with Arthur. One hour on the clock, but Arthur-time stretched and bent, like a solo that refused to end.

We sat in the back room of Rock School, a little cave stacked with amps, tangled cables, and towers of vinyl. Arthur had his notebook open, but the guitar across his lap was the real textbook.

He grinned at me. "Alright, Bodhi. First up: Robert Johnson's Cross Road Blues. Without him, you don't get modern guitar. Eric Clapton and Cream turned it into Crossroads. You'll play both, raw Delta blues, then full-throttle rock."

Colt twirled his sticks. "So, like, back-to-back?"

"Exactly," Arthur said, picking up his Strat. "Listen."

He slid his finger across the strings, no pick, just skin and steel. The note wailed, bending sharp then dropping flat, raw as a cry in the night. "That's Delta blues. Thumb on the bass strings, fingers dancing on top. The guitar is talking and walking at the same time."

I leaned forward. His thumb hammered a steady bass note, almost like a drum, while his other fingers picked the melody. Two parts. One person. My brain flipped.

Arthur winked. "Robert Johnson played it like two guitarists trapped in one body. That's the trick. Keep your thumb steady as a train, and let the fingers tell the story. Most kids quit when their thumb cramps up. Don't quit."

Then he clicked on a small amp, cranked the gain, and ripped into Clapton's Crossroads riff. The same bones, but now it roared. "Hear that? Same skeleton. Just plugged into the wall."

He set the guitar in my lap. "Your turn. Thumb steady. Don't let it drift."

I pressed the strings, nervous. My thumb stumbled after two bars, breaking rhythm.

"Stop," Arthur said gently. He leaned closer. "Here's a trick only players figure out the hard way, don't strangle the neck. Let the guitar breathe. Rest your hand, don't choke it. The blues is a conversation, not a wrestling match."

I tried again, loosening my grip. The bass notes thumped steadier, the melody a little freer. Not perfect. But better.

Arthur smiled. "There you go. That's the river talking."

He flipped the notebook. "Second pairing: B.B. King's The Thrill Is Gone, matched with Zeppelin's Since I've Been Loving You. Same emotion, different clothes. B.B. bends one note and you feel it in your bones."

He bent a string slowly, holding it so long I swear time stopped. "See? Don't rush a bend. Milk it. That's how you make the guitar sing instead of scream."

My stomach did a flip. Zeppelin. That was fire.

"Third: Muddy Waters' Hoochie Coochie Man. That riff, " He pounded out dun, dun-DUN on the low E. "That's swagger. The Stones stole the walk and never gave it back."

Jett grinned and echoed the riff on his bass. Arthur snapped his fingers, eyes sparkling.

"And last: Howlin' Wolf's Smokestack Lightning. Hypnotic. Gritty. Hendrix carried it into Voodoo Child. That'll be our closer. Wolf growls it, Hendrix sets it on fire."

He set his guitar across his lap, looking at each of us. "That's the setlist. Four pairs. Eight songs. By the time we're done, you'll not just play them, you'll feel the lineage under your fingers."

He tapped my strings one more time. "Remember this, Bodhi: play with your hands, but also with your ears. Your hands will lie. Your ears won't."

I nodded, trying to file it away forever. Zeppelin. Hendrix. Stones. But also Robert Johnson, B.B. King, Muddy Waters, Howlin' Wolf. The whole family tree.

Colt tapped his sticks against his leg. Jett plucked a groove low and smooth.

And me? My thumb throbbed, but my grin was unstoppable.

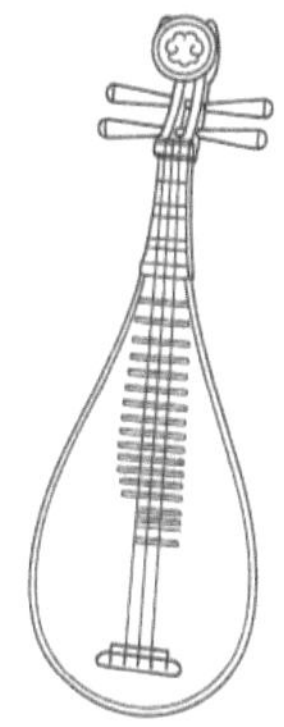

Chapter 34

The Pipa Lesson

On the way out, I asked Arthur if he had a few more minutes.

He leaned back in his chair, cracked his knuckles, and said, "Yeah, what's up? My last appointment canceled, so I'm good."

I shifted my guitar case nervously. "So… the Dragon Boat–Mid-Autumn Festival's coming up. I'm already rowing, doing Kung Fu forms, the lion dance… and now Mom signed me up to play the pipa. In front of, like, twelve… maybe eighteen thousand people."

Arthur raised an eyebrow. "Pipa, huh? Didn't know you had one."

I swallowed. Given to me by his daughter of an old master from who passed away. So, yeah... the expectations are kind of... huge."

Arthur sat up straighter. For once, the smile slid off his face. "That changes things."

"Tell me about it," I muttered. "I don't want to mess this up. I don't even know where to start. Do you have any advice? Like, how do I get good fast?"

Arthur studied me for a long moment, then leaned forward, elbows on his knees. His eyes sharpened like he was about to tell me something secret.

"Alright, kid. You want the truth? First thing: drown yourself in it. Don't just pluck it like a guitar in a new costume. Listen. Find the masters, Liu Fang, Wu Man, the legends. Play their recordings until you dream them. Slow them down if you have to, the way I slowed down my blues records. I'd drop a 45 to 33 rpm, pull every solo apart note by note. That's how I learned Clapton, Johnson, Hendrix.
Do the same with pipa. Let those sounds live in your bones."

"But how do I even know what I'm listening for?" I asked.

Arthur's voice softened. "The pipa isn't just notes. Every tune has a story. Take Ambush from Ten Sides. On paper it's a war epic. But on the strings? It's steel on steel, hoofbeats, chaos. You're not playing a melody. You're reenacting history. If you don't know the story, you'll just hit notes. Know the story, and you'll hit hearts."

I swallowed. "So, like, storytelling through sound."

"Exactly." Arthur pointed his finger like he was stabbing the air. "Respect the story, and the pipa will respect you back."

I tried to picture it. Playing war with strings. Pretty epic... and terrifying.

"But I'm a guitarist," I said. "Does that even help?"

Arthur chuckled, grabbed his Strat, and plucked a lazy blues run. "Kid, you've got a head start. Frets, strings, bends, you know the basics. But the pipa's got its own voice. Those endless tremolo rolls? They're like flamenco mixed with thunder. Harmonics that shimmer like glass. You can use your guitar ear, but don't force it. Adapt. Think of it like learning a new accent, you don't forget English, but you've got to respect the new tongue."

He leaned closer. "And loosen your grip. Don't choke it. Same lesson I gave you with guitar, only doubled. Let it sing. The second you strangle the strings, it'll sound like a toy instead of a soul."

I nodded, then asked, "Okay, but... how do you even know all this? You've never taught pipa."

Arthur smirked and leaned back, eyes going a little far away. "Ah. That takes me back. London. Seventies. I was playing pubs for peanuts, half-starved most nights. Met this girl, Li Mei. She played the pipa like it was breathing. Fingers flying so fast I thought the strings would melt. First time I saw her, it was at a Chinese cultural festival. Everyone else was chatting and drinking tea, and she made the room go silent with one song."

He chuckled. "We dated for a while. She made me sit on the floor while she practiced, told me stories about each piece, poetry, opera, battles, legends. I didn't understand half of it, but I felt it. She taught me that instruments aren't just sounds. They're carriers of memory. I learned enough to mess around on the pipa, but more than that? I learned respect. It's not a guitar with funny tuning, it's its own universe. That's what I'm passing to you."

I couldn't help grinning. "So you learned pipa… to impress a girl?"

Arthur barked out a laugh. "Kid, half of what I learned in music was chasing a girl. But that one stuck. Li Mei's gone now, but the lesson remains: treat the instrument as a whole world, not a trick."

I fiddled with my case. "But I don't have years. I have weeks."

Arthur leaned forward again, serious now. "Then play with purpose. No random fiddling. Every time you pick it up, set a goal. One run, one roll, one piece. Record yourself. Play it back. Be brutal, ask if it sings or clunks. Fix it. Don't just drill scales. Scales are push-ups. Songs are the fight. And you're stepping into the ring in front of twelve thousand people."

That made my stomach do a nosedive.

Arthur softened, his grin returning. "But remember: the crowd won't remember if you hit every note. They'll remember if you made them feel something. Trust your ear. Trust your gut. The pipa doesn't demand perfection, just honesty."

I hesitated. "So… you really think I can do this?"

He gave me a sideways grin, that rocker grin that looked like it had seen a thousand smoky bars. "Kid, you've got grit. You fight your thumb till it cramps, then show up hungry for more. You honor the old master by showing up, by trying, by feeling it. Do that, and you won't just play the pipa. You'll carry it forward."

I laughed nervously. "So basically… don't suck, but also be legendary?"

Arthur winked. "Now you're catching on."

Chapter 35
Grasshopper

The morning was a blur. Math, science, locker jam, almost-late-to-class sprint, it all mixed together like one giant swirl. By the time lunch finally rolled around, I felt like I'd been through three sparring rounds with Sifu Huang.

I pulled out my lunch from my backpack and set it on the table. Same thing as always: a little container of rice, a strip of roasted seaweed, and apple slices. Not exciting, but predictable. At least I knew what I was getting.

A minute later, Riley slid onto the bench across from me. She unpacked her own food too, sliced fruit, raw vegetables, and a few crackers. Definitely no pizza or mystery meat like half the cafeteria had.

"Hey, Bodhi," she said, grinning. "I see you're rocking Linkin Park today."

I looked down at my shirt and smirked. "Yeah. And you've got INXS. Respect. That's cool."

And she was cool. Riley had that whole effortless vibe going, shoulder-length dirty-blonde hair, jeans, and a vintage rocker T-shirt that looked like it had been through a real concert, not just pulled off a store rack. She made it look easy.

Then she tilted her head at me. "Huh. I see you had gardening class today."

I frowned. "Uh… yeah. Why?"

"Don't move."

Those two words froze me solid. "Wait, what? Don't move? That's not something you just say to a person at lunch! What's in my hair?!"

She leaned across the table, her face so close I could smell something citrusy in her shampoo, and carefully plucked something out of my hair. When she pulled her hand back, there was a tiny green bug squirming in her palm.

"Oh no way," I groaned. "That's been crawling around since gardening class?"

"Looks like it," Riley said, laughing softly. She cupped it carefully. "I'll be right back."

And then she just walked straight out of the cafeteria, holding the bug like it was a VIP.

When she came back, I asked, "Okay, seriously. Where'd you go?"

"To put it in the grass," she said matter-of-factly. "I didn't want to kill it. That's kind of my Buddhist thing. I don't know a ton about Buddhism yet, but… I feel like I shouldn't hurt stuff if I don't have to."

I blinked. "No way. My family's Buddhist too."

Riley smiled like she already knew. "Yeah. I could tell."

"You could tell? How?"

Riley just shrugged, smooth as ever. "I can just tell."

And suddenly, right there in the middle of the noisy cafeteria, I felt like Riley had just peeked into my brain and read a page.

"Oh then, you would love meeting my mom," I said. "She's all about talking Aumé-Buddhism. She's even going to have a booth at the Dragon Boat Festival. She's looking for volunteers."

Riley grinned. "Cool. Count me in."

"Really? She would love that."

"So, how's it going with the Dragon Boat Festival and all that stuff you've got going on there?"

I took a deep breath. "Honestly? I feel a little better about it."

Her eyebrow went up like she didn't totally believe me.

"Yesterday I had a lesson with Arthur, you know, my guitar instructor, and we actually made some progress on our sets for Rock House. That part felt good, like I could finally see the songs coming together.

And the crazy thing is, Arthur knew a little bit about the pipa too. Not a lot, but enough to help me figure out some scales and how the fingerings worked. It was kind of wild hearing him connect guitar riffs to pipa runs."

Like, here's this ancient instrument, and suddenly we're jamming on blues progressions together. He even showed me how blues patterns could shift over. It was wild, like, one second it's ancient Chinese music, the next second it's practically B.B. King. For a minute I thought, okay, maybe I can do this." It made me feel like maybe I wasn't totally lost."

Riley smiled. "That does sound cool."

"Yeah," I said. "But even with that, I'm still stressed. There's just so much. The rowing. The Kung Fu demos. The lion dance. The pipa. It feels like my brain is running four marathons at once."

"So how do your parents say you should deal with it?" Riley asked

I hesitated. "Well… my dad's a music director for a big star."

Her eyes widened. "Seriously? Which one?"

"Can't say." I shook my head. "It's not just a family rule. It's legal. Like NDA legal. We literally aren't allowed to talk about it."

"Mum's the word," she said, pretending to zip her lips shut.

"Yeah. But because of that, Dad knows what it's like to handle huge pressure. Tours, recordings, last-minute changes, he's always in the middle of chaos. And he tells me the same thing every time: break things down into smaller pieces.

"Don't stare at the whole mountain. Just pick one step and take it."

"And when you're on that step, you don't think about the others. You just do that one."

"I poked at my rice with my chopsticks. "It sounds simple. But it's not. Not when all the steps are screaming at you at once."

"And your mom," Riley asked, crunching on a carrot stick, "how does she think you should manage it all?"

I thought about it for a second. "Well… my mom follows Aumé-Buddhism. It's kind of like walking the Buddhist path but also recognizing the spirit, sort of how Christianity has the Holy Spirit, but in a Buddhist way."

Riley nodded slowly, listening.

"Her way of dealing with stuff is connecting to Aumé each morning and asking the question: How? Whatever it is you're facing, you just ask How?"

I leaned forward, trying to explain it the way Mom always did. "So, like in my situation right now, I'd wake up and ask, How can I manage Rock School practice, the pipa set, regular school and homework, Kung Fu, remember all of the Lion Dance routine, and somehow make it all fit together?"

I gave a little laugh. "It's not like Aumé sends you a text with the answer. But Mom says if you stay aware, if you pay attention, the answers show up in your day. Maybe in a conversation, or in the way something clicks while you're practicing, or even in the mistakes. But you've got to be awake enough to notice."

Riley tilted her head. "So the answers are already there. You just have to see them?"

"Exactly."

She smiled. "Pretty cool".

I paused, staring at my half-eaten apple slice. "You know what? I just realized something. With everything going on, I'm always talking about me, my music, my training, my stress." I looked up at her. "Sorry about that. Right now, I want to know about you."

Riley blinked, like she wasn't expecting me to say that. Then the corners of her mouth curled into a small smile.

"So... were you born here, or where are you from?" I asked.

Riley rested her chin on her hand. "Nah, I wasn't born here. I'm from Oregon. My family moved down to Texas a couple of years ago. My dad got a new job, and my mom wanted to be closer to her sister."

"So that accounts for the cool Northwest sort of vibe," I said with a grin.

Before Riley could answer, the bell rang, cutting through the cafeteria noise.

"Darn," I muttered, stuffing my lunch back into my backpack. "Tomorrow at lunch is officially Get to Know Riley day."

I paused for half a second, then added, "Date?"

Her eyes went wide for a second, then she smirked. "You bet."

We both turned red, just a little.

And that's when the Old Monk's voice drifted into my head: "The tongue often runs ahead of the heart, but sometimes it knows the path before you do."

Chapter 36

Lion and the Rabbits

Tuesday night was Kung Fu night, and Mom dropped Sid and me off at the studio. The place always smelled like sweat, tiger balm, and the faint rubber of the training mats. The second we bowed at the door, Sifu's eyes locked on us like he was already measuring our effort for the night.

"Line up!" he called.

We snapped into rows. The workout began the way it always did, with warm-ups that were really just disguised torture. Jogging in place, high knees, push-ups, sit-ups, mountain climbers, then stretching until my shoulders cracked. By the end of it, I was already dripping with sweat, and class hadn't even started yet.

Next came basics. Sifu barked commands, his voice sharp as a drumbeat. "Front punch! Rising block! Roundhouse kick!" The room echoed with the snap of uniforms and the slap of bare feet on the mat. My arms felt like rubber bands by the fifteenth punch, but I tried to keep each strike crisp. The green belt around my waist wasn't just decoration. Sid, still in orange, worked just as hard, though I could tell his form was getting sloppy when he got tired. His roundhouse almost looked sharp. Almost.

Then forms. Sifu split us up, greens and above on one side, oranges and yellows on the other. He had Sid's group drilling their first full form, correcting stances and reminding them to breathe with every strike. My group worked on a longer, more complex set. "A form is a fight against ten opponents," Sifu reminded us as he circled. "Show me all ten."

I tried to imagine them coming at me from every direction, ducking, blocking, countering. Sweat ran down my back, stinging my eyes, but I pushed through, keeping my stances low and strong. For a few seconds at a time, it felt real, like I was moving inside a story instead of just copying a sequence of moves.

Finally, weapons. Tonight was staff training. The sound of wood filled the studio, whip, crack, thump, as we drilled spins, strikes, and blocks. I loved the rhythm of it, the way the staff whistled through the air when I got the speed right. Sid wobbled through his turns, nearly losing his grip, but Sifu was right there, steadying his hands. "Grip with purpose. Control the weapon, or the weapon controls you."

The floor shook as we stepped forward together, staffs striking downward, then snapping back into guard. My arms ached, my legs shook, but in a good way, the kind of pain that proved you were getting stronger.

We ended the workout standing in horse stance, legs bent, fists at our sides, the whole class breathing heavy. My thighs burned like fire. I wanted to collapse. Instead, I stayed rooted, staring straight ahead.

"Relax," Sifu finally said. "Sit."

We sank down, legs crossed, backs straight. That's when I knew it was one of those nights. Sometimes class ended right there, just the workout. But other times, Sifu closed with something else. A talk. A reminder. A story.

Tonight, he paced slowly in front of us, hands behind his back. His eyes scanned the class, pausing here and there like he was seeing things we didn't even know we were showing.

"I watched you tonight," he began. "Some of you gave everything. Some of you struggled. Some of you doubted yourselves. That is normal. What matters is what you do with it."

The room was silent except for our breathing.

"Commitment," Sifu said. "It is easy to say yes. It is harder to honor yes."

My stomach twisted. Whoa.

"Anyone can promise. Not everyone delivers. Commitment is a test, not of strength, not of skill, but of perseverance. Do you keep showing up? Do you keep working when you are tired, when you are sore, when your mind says, 'I cannot?'" He tapped his temple. "This is where you win or lose."

I felt my chest tighten. He couldn't know about the Dragon Boat Festival, about everything I'd piled on my plate, the rowing, the Kung Fu demos, the lion dance, the pipa performance. But it was like he was talking straight to me anyway.

Sifu stopped pacing. His eyes seemed to land on mine. "When you face many things at once, do not scatter your mind. A lion does not chase ten rabbits. A lion chooses one."

I swallowed hard. That sounded a lot like what Dad always said about "chunking it out." But hearing it here, from Sifu, hit different.

He went on. "Respect your commitments. To others, yes. But also to yourself. If you doubt yourself, you weaken your spirit. If you believe, if you keep going, then your spirit carries you forward, even when your body is tired."

I stared at the mat, his words pounding in my head louder than the drum at lion dance practice.

Sifu folded his arms. "Some of you tonight showed respect to your classmates. Helping them. Encouraging them. That is also commitment. Because when we commit, we do not commit alone. We commit together."

My throat felt tight. I thought about Riley, about May in lion dance, about Arthur in Rock School, about everyone who was trusting me to show up. It wasn't just about me juggling everything. It was about not letting them down.

Finally, Sifu clasped his hands. "So. Remember this. Commitment is not a burden. It is an honor. If you treat it like a weight, it will crush you. If you treat it like a gift, it will lift you."

The room stayed quiet. I breathed in, heavy and slow, and for the first time in days, the swirl of worry in my chest eased up. Not gone. But lighter. Clearer.

The Old Monk chuckled in my mind, 'When the head is heavy with worry, bow lower. Worry will roll off like a melon.'

Chapter 37
Ocean Cove

Riley walked up behind me and said, "Nope, no critters today."

I laughed. "Ha! I had gardening again, but we're actually seeding now. Hoping for a winter harvest in early December."

"Nice," she said, sliding onto the bench across from me.

I set out my lunch, rice, seaweed, and apple slices. She unpacked hers: fruit, raw vegetables, and some crackers. Simple.

"But today," I said, pointing a chopstick at her, "is your day. I've been talking about myself nonstop. I want to know more about Riley."

She tilted her head, pretending to think. "Same-same as always."

I shook my head. "Nope. Not allowed. That's my line. Your turn."

She smiled, giving in. "Okay… well, my dad works in tech. Computers, coding, all that. He's the serious one in the family. Like, the kind of guy who'll spend an entire Saturday fixing one tiny glitch on his laptop and act like it's the world's most important mission. He doesn't laugh much, but when he does, it's usually at some nerdy joke none of us get.

"And now he's into crypto. Bitcoin, Ethereum, all the altcoins, you name it. He checks prices on his phone like ten times an hour. He's convinced the whole world's going to run on blockchain one day, money, government, even schools. He says it so seriously, like he's predicting the future. Half the time it just sounds like another language."

She picked up a slice of apple, then added, "My mom's the opposite. She's really into yoga. Not into mainstream religion, but yoga is her thing. She's always trying to drag me off to these yoga retreats. And honestly… yeah, they're kind of fun. They keep you in shape, and they make you more aware of what you're eating and how you're living. Thus the carrot." Riley crunched on one of her carrot sticks, grinning.

"But she's also more of a seeker. Always reading, everything from old philosophy books to new-age stuff about energy and healing. She says she doesn't have all the answers, but she loves the search. Sometimes I catch her just sitting quietly, like she's waiting for the universe to tell her something.

"And she loves to garden. Vegetables, flowers, herbs, you name it. She says digging in the dirt is her way of listening to the earth. Hey, when you guys meet, you can talk about gardening. She'd love that."

The words slipped out, and Riley froze, realizing what she'd said. Her cheeks went pink. "I mean, if you ever did meet her."

I grinned but didn't say anything, just let her squirm a little before she hurried on.

"And then there's Jack, my brother. He's a sophomore at Twin Lakes. He's mostly into soccer, plays on the school team, spends a ton of time practicing. He messes around on guitar too, but mostly just messing. Not amazing or anything. Sometimes I pick up a little from him, like a chord or a riff, but he's more likely to be outside kicking a ball than sitting inside practicing scales."

"Soccer and guitar," I said. "Not bad."

She smirked. "Yeah, he thinks he's cooler than he is."

For a moment, we ate in silence, the cafeteria buzzing around us. Then I asked, "Do you miss Oregon?"

Her face softened. "Yeah. Especially the coast. The ocean was always there, huge, endless, alive. It made everything else feel… smaller."

She leaned forward, lowering her voice. "Once, I went down to the shore by myself. Didn't tell anyone I was going. It was this little cove at the bottom of a cliff. You had to walk down this long wooden staircase. At the bottom, you were surrounded by cliffs, and in front of you, the ocean."

"The waves came rolling in, crashing and foaming, then pulling back with this sound like the whole earth was breathing. The water stretched out forever, and I felt… tiny. Like nothing I worried about mattered compared to something that big. And I remember thinking, if a rogue wave came and filled that cove, it would sweep me away. Since I hadn't told anyone I was there, no one would even know what happened. It would be like I never existed. And I wondered… would anyone even miss me?"

For a moment, the cafeteria noise blurred away, and it was just Riley, the cliffs, and the endless pull of the tide.

"Well," I said softly, "I'm glad there was no rogue wave. Because otherwise, you wouldn't be here today."

Without thinking, I reached over and placed my hand on hers. "And I've heard you sing. Girl, you rock. And we need you in the band."

Her cheeks flushed again, but she smiled, squeezing my hand lightly before pulling back.

The bell rang, sharp and sudden.

Chapter 38

The Pick Drops

House Rock was at five o'clock sharp. By the time I got there, everyone else was already unpacking, except Riley. She slipped in about five minutes late, carrying her guitar and flashing a quick smile like she was trying not to look guilty.

Jeff, our director, clapped his hands once, loud enough to cut through the tuning and chatter. "Alright, listen up. We're starting with the first pair. Robert Johnson's Cross Road Blues. Without him, you don't get modern guitar, period. Then we'll jump to Eric Clapton and Cream's Crossroads. Two sides of the same coin. You'll play both, raw Delta blues first, then full-throttle rock."

He scanned the room like a hawk making sure we got it. "And don't just play the notes. I want you to hear the dirt roads in Johnson's version, the deal with the devil kind of ache. Then, when you hit Cream's version, I want the amps roaring, like you're standing on a festival stage in front of fifty thousand people."

I swallowed. No pressure, right?

We launched into Cross Road Blues first. At least, that's what it was supposed to be. I tried to keep the slide licks gritty, but my timing kept slipping. The drummer lost the shuffle halfway through. The bass line came in too heavy, more rock than blues. And when Riley added her guitar fills, they clashed with mine, like two people arguing in different languages.

It didn't feel raw and haunted. It just felt messy.

We limped into the final turnaround, all of us staring at our instruments like they might apologize for us.

Jeff didn't clap. He didn't smile. He just stood there with his arms crossed. That was worse than yelling.

"Alright," he said finally, his voice cutting like sandpaper. "What was that?"

No one answered.

He paced in front of us, shaking his head. "You can't fake blues. You can't rush it, you can't paste rock attitude on it, and you definitely can't play it like you're half-asleep. Robert Johnson played like his soul was on the line, because maybe it was. You? You sounded like a garage band trying to remember their chords."

I felt my ears burning. He was right. It hadn't just been sloppy, it had been empty.

Jeff jabbed a finger toward us. "Music is storytelling. If you don't believe the story, nobody else will. Right now, I don't believe a word you're playing."

The silence was heavy. Someone coughed. Riley's eyes stayed glued to her guitar, her cheeks red.

Jeff let the words hang a moment longer, then clapped his hands again. "Second pairing. The Thrill Is Gone by B.B. King, matched with Led Zeppelin's Since I've Been Loving You. Same emotion, different clothes. One aches, the other wails. Let's see if you can do better this time."

Jeff clapped his hands again. "Second pairing. The Thrill Is Gone by B.B. King, matched with Led Zeppelin's Since I've Been Loving You. Same emotion, different clothes. One aches, the other wails. Let's go."

We settled back in. I tried to center myself, imagining B.B. King leaning over Lucille, his guitar practically singing the pain out of his chest. Our drummer counted us in, slow, steady, and for a few bars, it almost worked. The bass line laid down a groove, the notes hung heavy, and Riley's chords draped across it like a shadow.

Then I came in. My solo was supposed to float, mournful, but I couldn't find the space. I filled too much, too fast, and it just sounded busy. Our drummer overcompensated, hitting harder, and suddenly the ache turned into clatter. By the time we limped out of the last chorus, the song had lost its soul.

Jeff pinched the bridge of his nose. "No. No, no, no. The Thrill Is Gone isn't about notes, it's about silence. The space between the notes. You can't crowd it. You have to let it breathe." He pointed at me. "When you play that solo, I want you to imagine your heart breaking in slow motion. Drag it out. Make us wait for the note. If you can't stand the silence, you don't understand the blues."

I nodded, but my stomach twisted.

Jeff didn't wait long. "Fine. Let's crank it. Zeppelin."

We launched into Since I've Been Loving You. I tried to shake off the nerves, channel Jimmy Page's unhinged bends and wild sustain. The drummer went for bombast this time, and the bass thundered. Riley's rhythm work was solid, and her voice came in rawer, more desperate. For a moment, I thought, maybe this is it.

But then we lost it again. The drummer rushed the fills. Riley's timing slipped when she tried to match the phrasing of the original. My solo went sideways, one bend too sharp, then another, and instead of wailing, it just squealed. We crashed into the ending like a car with no brakes.

Jeff sighed, loud enough for all of us to hear. "Better than the first pair, but that's not saying much." He paced the room like a lion in a cage. "Blues and blues-rock, two different languages. B.B. King whispers, Jimmy Page screams, but both are telling you the same thing: love hurts, and it's not going away. If you don't feel that, if you don't mean it, the audience will know. And right now, you're playing like kids copying homework."

No one dared argue. He let the silence drag, then pointed to the set list taped on the wall. "We've got more pairings to run. You're not close. Not yet. Let's go."

And that's how it went. For the next two-plus hours, we stumbled through song after song, Jeff stopping us, dissecting us, drilling us, pushing us past the point where my fingers ached and the calluses on my fretting hand burned. Every mistake echoed in my head. Every sideways glance between bandmates said the same thing, we weren't practicing enough on our own.

When Jeff finally called it, we left knowing it. No sugarcoating. No pep talk. Just a clear message: if we wanted to be ready for Rock House, we had to work harder. A lot harder.

Outside afterward, I slung my guitar case over my shoulder, the night air cool against my sweaty shirt. Riley walked up beside me, her face still a little flushed from rehearsal.

"I think we need to practice," she said quietly. "You want to get together on Saturday? I know it'll help me a lot."

I was tired, drained, my fingers sore. But hearing her say that was like the one bright spot in a long, bruising evening.

"Yeah," I said. "Saturday."

The old monk chuckle: "Even the hardest stones are shaped drop by drop. But only if they let the water keep falling."

Chapter 39

Carrots and Apple Slices

I dropped my container of rice, seaweed, and apple slices onto the table and slid onto the bench with a sigh. A minute later, Riley showed up with her usual, fruit, veggie sticks, and crackers. She sat across from me, setting her lunch down without a word, then gave me one of those half-grins that said she was about to bring something up.

"So," she said, crunching a cracker, "were we really that bad last night?"

I poked at my rice with my chopsticks, stalling. "Yes. We were that bad."

Her smile drooped, and she sank a little lower in her seat.

"But not as bad as my first band back in Oceanside," I added quickly. "We were awful. The neighbors actually nicknamed us the Dead Cats."

Her head shot up. "The Dead Cats?"

"Yep. Because that's what we sounded like. Even the neighborhood cats would scatter whenever we practiced."

Riley burst out laughing, covering her mouth so carrot bits wouldn't fly. "That's brutal."

"Brutally accurate," I said. "So yeah, we were bad last night, but trust me, we weren't Dead Cats bad."

She shook her head, still grinning. "Okay, fair. But good thing we're practicing on Saturday. If we can up our game, I bet the others will step up too."

"Agreed," I said.

For a moment, we both ate quietly. The noise of the cafeteria filled the space, kids shouting across tables, sneakers squeaking, the occasional clang of a dropped tray. I could tell Riley was replaying Jeff's critique in her head, just like I was. Music is storytelling. If you don't believe the story, nobody else will. He hadn't been wrong.

Riley suddenly sat up straighter, like she'd decided to change the subject before we both spiraled into despair. "So… how's gardening going?"

I chuckled. "It's going. We're planting now."

"What are you planting?"

I counted on my fingers. "Cabbage, carrots, radishes, kale, spinach, bok choy… pretty much all the fall stuff."

Riley wrinkled her nose. "Radishes? Hard pass. But spinach? Yes. Kale? Maybe. Depends how you cook it."

"You don't cook kale," I said. "You survive it."

That made her laugh again, and some of the heaviness from practice finally started to lift.

I bit into an apple slice, savoring the crisp snap. Riley crunched on a carrot stick, loud enough that I could hear it over the cafeteria buzz. For a moment, it was just us, eating in rhythm.

"Oh, by the way," Riley said after a pause. "For Saturday, do you want to come to my house or yours?"

I thought about it. My house would mean Sid hanging around, probably "accidentally" strumming my guitar and begging to join in. But then I remembered Mom and the Aumé-Buddhism booth at the Mid-Autumn Festival.

"Well," I said, "since you wanted to talk about volunteering at the Aumé-Buddhism booth at the Mid-Autumn Festival, I thought you could come to my house. Mom wants to meet you anyway."

Riley's eyes widened just a little. "Oh… you told her about me?"

I felt my cheeks heat up. "Yeah."

She blushed too, then smiled. "Okay."

The bell rang, and just like that, the cafeteria dissolved into chaos. Chairs scraped, kids scrambled, and the noise level shot through the roof.

Riley stood, slinging her bag over her shoulder. "Saturday," she said.

"Saturday," I echoed, packing away the last of my rice.

Chapter 40
Water Safety

Sometimes you get verification that Aumé, or the universe, or something, is actually listening.

Like when you're talking with your friends about skateboards, and the next time you open your phone, there are five ads for skateboards waiting for you. Coincidence? Or creepy Siri magic? Things that make you go hummm.

After lunch with Riley, I had Pioneering class. Up until now, we'd covered knot-tying and lashing, campfire building, and even outdoor cooking. Useful, sure. But now, exactly two weeks before I'm supposed to paddle in an actual Dragon Boat race, what do we get? Boat and water safety.

Coincidence?

Either way, I wasn't complaining.

Our teacher, Mr. Daniels, was the kind of guy who looked like he'd been carved out of a state park. Tanned skin, arms that could probably bench-press a canoe, and this booming voice that could make even the loudest middle schoolers shut up. His beard always looked a little windblown, like he lived in a tent and the outdoors was his barber.

"Alright, pioneers!" he barked, clapping his hands. "Today's the big one. Water safety. Life jackets, balance drills, paddle technique, and if we've got time, capsize recovery. By the end of class, you'll know how not to drown. Important life skill, wouldn't you say?"

A few kids snorted. Someone muttered, "More important than algebra."

"Correct," Mr. Daniels said without missing a beat. "Grab your gear."

We marched down to Twin Lakes, the sun bouncing off the water like it was showing off. Ducks paddled by, eyeing us suspiciously. The dock was lined with aluminum rowboats, their metal sides glinting. Beside them, a rack of bright orange life jackets waited, smelling like sunscreen and chlorine had a baby.

"Lesson one," Mr. Daniels said, tossing a jacket to the kid in front. "Always wear a life jacket. Doesn't matter if you think you're Michael Phelps. Water doesn't care. Life jackets save lives. Period."

He strapped one on, tugging the buckles tight. "It should feel snug. Not so snug you pass out, but close. Pair up and check each other's straps."

I got paired with Hunter, the human safety manual. He yanked my straps so tight I squeaked.

"Dude, I need to breathe," I wheezed.

"Safety first," Hunter replied, deadly serious.

When it was my turn, I loosened his straps just enough so he wouldn't explode. He gave me the stink-eye but didn't fix them.

"Now," Mr. Daniels said, "let's talk balance. Boats are not sidewalks. You can't stomp in, flop down, and expect nothing to happen. Treat them with respect. Boats are like people, they get cranky if you don't."

That got a laugh. He waved us toward the boats. "Climb in carefully, one at a time. Low and centered. Ninja, not elephant. Go."

The first few kids made it look easy, sliding in smooth. Then came Jacob. Jacob thought he was the class comedian. He leapt into the boat like he was diving into an action movie, arms wide, knees bent. SPLASH. The boat flipped, dumping him into the water.

He came up sputtering, laughing like it was the funniest thing in the world.

Mr. Daniels blew his whistle. "And that, class, is what not to do. Thank you, Jacob, for your demonstration."

We all clapped, and Jacob bowed from the water.

Next came paddles. Mr. Daniels held his like it was a magic staff. "This is not an oar, not a drumstick, and definitely not a lightsaber. Paddles are extensions of your arms. Treat them right, and they'll move you where you want to go."

He dipped the paddle in the water and pulled, smooth as silk. His boat glided like it was on invisible tracks.

We tried. Chaos. Half the class splashed more water than they moved. One boat spun in circles. Another nearly collided with the dock. Hunter barked "Form! Form!" at me every time I tried to put some muscle into it.

"Relax, man," I told him. "We're not storming Normandy."

"Balance!" he barked back, glaring.

At one point, I leaned away from his paddle and almost tipped us both. Mr. Daniels' whistle shrieked.

"Bodhi! What do we say about leaning?"

"Uh… treat the boat with respect?" I called.

"Correct! Gold star for you. Minus two for style."

The class cracked up. Even I had to laugh.

Then came the "man overboard" drill. Mr. Daniels tossed an orange buoy into the lake. "Person overboard! Rescue!"

Instant chaos. Boats zigzagged like bumper cars. Kids pointed, shouted, and leaned dangerously close to tipping. Hunter leaned out so far I thought he'd be the next "overboard," but somehow he hooked the buoy with his paddle and dragged it in.

"Excellent," Mr. Daniels said. "Now imagine it's your best friend. Do you want to be the one who fumbles, or the one who knows what to do?"

We all got quiet. Even Jacob.

"Exactly," he said, softer now. "Respect the water, and it'll respect you."

By the end, we were soaked, sore, and buzzing. My arms ached, my shoes squished, and my brain felt like it had just downloaded an entire boating manual.

Coincidence or not, it felt like the universe had given me exactly the training I needed.

Chapter 41

The Side Kick

Friday night at Kung Fu class always felt different. Maybe it was the hum in the air from everyone being tired after a week of school, or maybe it was just the knowledge that sparring was coming. Whatever it was, you could practically feel the electricity buzzing on the mats.

Mom dropped Sid and me off as usual, and we changed into our uniforms. Sid was bouncing around like he'd just downed three sodas, while I was trying to look calm, green belt tied just right, like a guy who'd been around the block.

We warmed up, jogging in circles, high knees, push-ups, then endless stretching. My legs burned, but Sifu Huang's voice kept us steady. "Breath controls movement. Don't rush the breath."

After drills, punches, blocks, stances, it was time. "Sparring," Sifu Huang announced. The whole class perked up, some nervous, some grinning.

Pairs formed. I wasn't surprised when Sifu called, "Bodhi and Sid."

I smirked. Easy match. I was taller, older, stronger. Green belt to his orange. What could he possibly do?

We bowed to each other, then to Sifu. "Respect first, skill second," Sifu reminded us.

Sid squared up in his stance, eyes wide and serious. I could barely keep a straight face. He looked like a six-year-old pretending to be Bruce Lee.

We circled. I tossed out a light jab, testing him. He blocked. Not bad. I flicked a lazy kick. He slid away, almost grinning.

"Not bad, little bro," I teased.

His eyes narrowed. He wasn't smiling anymore.

The next second, BAM! Sid's foot shot up in a clean side kick, straight into my stomach. The impact knocked the air out of me. I staggered back, clutching my middle, eyes wide.

The whole class gasped.

For a moment, Sid froze, like maybe he'd gone too far. Then his face exploded into the biggest grin I'd ever seen. "I got you!" he yelled, bouncing on his toes.

The kids cracked up, some clapping. Even Sifu Huang chuckled.

"Good control, Sid," Sifu said. "Clean strike, correct distance. Bodhi, " his eyes found mine, still bent over and wheezing, "never underestimate an opponent, no matter their size or rank. Pride blinds faster than a punch."

The lesson stung more than Sid's kick. But it was true.

We continued sparring. This time I wasn't fooling around. Sid came at me with sharp little punches and kicks, faster than I expected. I blocked, countered, and landed a few, but he made me work for it. He wasn't just playing anymore, he was learning. He was dangerous.

When Sifu finally called, "Time," we bowed again, breathing hard. Sid's face was glowing, sweat dripping, but he still looked like he could do ten more rounds.

As we walked off the mat, he jabbed me right where his kick had landed. "Perfect angle, right? You didn't even see it coming!"

I groaned. "Yeah, Sid. I noticed."

On the ride home, he wouldn't stop talking. "Did you see how clean it was? My foot landed just right. I kept my guard up, too. And the balance! Sifu always says balance is everything, and I had it! Did you see?"

"Yes, Sid," I said, staring out the window.

But inside? I couldn't help smiling. He'd earned every bit of that excitement. And for the first time, I realized I was going to have to stop treating my little brother like a little brother on the mat.

Because Sid wasn't just tagging along anymore. Sid was coming for me.

Chapter 42

Making Dumplings

At exactly eleven o'clock, the knock came. I was halfway down the hall when I heard Sid's sneakers thundering across the wood floor.

"I got it!" he shouted, like the door was some prize to be claimed.

By the time I caught up, he was already yanking it open.

"Hi, " Sid froze mid-word, blinking. It wasn't just Riley standing there. Next to her was a taller guy, maybe sixteen or seventeen, with the same sandy-blond hair but a little longer, shaggy under a baseball cap. Keys jingled in his hand.

"This is Jack," Riley said, rolling her eyes. "My brother. He insisted on dropping me off."

"Checking to make sure all was all right," Jack added, giving me and the house a quick once-over like some undercover security agent.

Mom, appeared behind me, wiping her hands on a dish towel. Perfect timing. "Hello! I'm Lily Dharma. Come in, both of you."

Jack shook his head. "Thanks, but I've got soccer practice. Just wanted to make sure Riley was good."

I stepped forward, offering my hand. "I'm Bodhi."

Jack gave it a firm shake, his expression that classic big-brother mix of protective and skeptical. "Cool," he said finally.

Mom smiled warmly. "Nice to meet you, Jack. Don't worry, Riley's in good hands here, but you're a good broteher to do that and make sure."

That seemed to relax him a little. "Okay then. Just… take good care of my sister."

"Jack!" Riley hissed, mortified.

He grinned, backing away toward the driveway where his beat-up Honda was idling. "Later, Riley. Nice to meet you all."

When the door clicked shut, Sid was still planted at Riley's side, and I realized he was holding her hand like some kind of junior chaperone.

As we walked into the living room, he puffed up and asked, "So, Riley, are you Bodhi's girlfriend?" He looked at me with a sly grin, like he'd just set off a firecracker.

I froze, mid-step, heat climbing my neck.

Riley didn't even blink. She looked Sid square in the eye and said, "Yes. In fact, we're getting married next Saturday. How about you being the best man?"

Sid's mouth fell open. He just stood there, stunned into silence, blinking like a cartoon character.

Lily covered her mouth, shoulders shaking with laughter. I just about choked trying not to laugh.

Riley held her poker face for another beat before winking at me. That did it, I cracked up. Mom laughed out loud too.

Sid stomped his foot. "You guys are messing with me!"

"Of course we are," Riley said, ruffling his hair. "But you'd make an awesome best man."

Sid tried to glare, but it melted into a grin.

Mom smiled at Riley and said, "Come on into the kitchen. I thought we could make some dumplings and talk about the Dragon Boat Festival. I understand you might help at the Aumé-Buddhism booth."

The kitchen was already alive when we walked in. Bowls of filling sat on the counter, ginger, scallions, cabbage, a touch of soy, while a neat stack of round dumpling wrappers rested under a damp towel. The smell made Sid hover like a moth over a porch light.

"Any girl who's a friend of Bodhi needs to know how to make dumplings," Mom said with a grin.

"Mom," I groaned, dragging a hand down my face.

Riley laughed nervously, then tucked her hair behind her ear. "I've never made dumplings before. This is new for me."

"Perfect," Mom said. She washed her hands, then showed Riley how to spoon just enough filling onto the wrapper, fold it over, and pinch the edges shut with little pleats. "It's all about balance. Too much filling, it bursts. Too little, it's empty. Just right, and it holds together."

Riley copied her, clumsy at first, but Mom nodded. "Good. You'll get the feel of it."

Sid leaned on the counter. "Can I watch?"

"Of course," Mom said. "After we make them, we'll have some lunch. Then Sid and I will give you two some space to practice."

That perked me up. Finally, music time. But for now, I leaned against the counter and watched the dumplings multiply like little crescents.

Mom's tone softened. "Bodhi's father and I have always been Buddhist, more as a way of being than a religion. We were against war, against violence. We became vegetarians because we believe in the sanctity of all living things. Buddhism felt like the right path for us. But still, something was missing, until we found Aumé-Buddhism."

Riley glanced up from her dumpling. "Okay… what's different about it?"

"Aumé-Buddhists acknowledge the spirit," Mom explained. "What in Christianity is called the Holy Spirit. At the core of every religion is the spirit, but too often it gets wrapped up in dogma and rules, in culture and community, until it becomes about who's in and who's out."

She set another dumpling on the tray. "Aumé-Buddhism is about uniting all of those connected to the spirit, whatever their culture, community, or tribe. And while connected to that spirit, we walk the Buddhist path, compassion, mindfulness, kindness. The practice grounds us, the spirit guides us."

Riley pinched her dumpling closed, this one cleaner than her first. "So it's not about having all the answers. It's about staying connected to that spark."

"Exactly," Mom said. "The answers are already there. We just need to quiet down enough to notice them."

Sid, still perched on his stool, tilted his head. "So Aumé is like… spirit Wi-Fi?"

I nearly dropped my guitar pick laughing. Riley snorted too. Mom sighed, but her eyes twinkled. "Maybe, Sid. Except this connection doesn't drop. Only people do."

Riley's smile widened. She looked down at the dumpling in her hand, like it suddenly meant something bigger than food.

Mom clapped her hands once, lightly. "Alright then, let's cook some dumplings and eat."

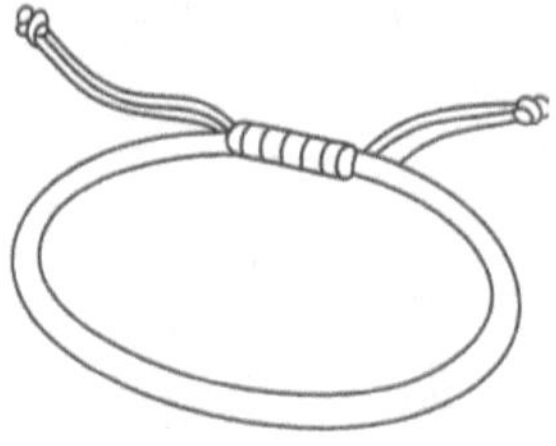

Chapter 43

Protection Strings

Mom showed Riley how to stack the dumplings into the bamboo steamer baskets, those pretty, woven ones that looked almost too nice to cook food in. Steam puffed up when the lid lifted, carrying the smell of ginger and garlic through the kitchen.

A few minutes later, we were seated around the table. Each of us had our own little basket in front of us, and there was a neat stack of extras in the middle for seconds. Sid dug in like he hadn't eaten in days. Riley picked up her first dumpling with chopsticks, a little awkward but determined, and popped it into her mouth. Her eyes went wide.

"These are amazing," she said after swallowing. "Like, seriously amazing."

Mom beamed. "Food is always better when you make it yourself."

We ate for a while, the room filled with the sound of chopsticks clicking against bamboo, until Riley set hers down and asked, "So… what exactly will I do at the booth?"

Mom wiped her hands gently on a napkin. "Most of the time, you'll be putting protection strings on the kids and people who come by. Each string will have a little card that explains what it is." She picked up one of the red threads from a small dish nearby, holding it between her fingers.

"These are usually called protection strings or blessing strings. In Sanskrit and Pali, they're called a *raksha sutra,* which literally means 'protection thread.' In Thai Buddhism, it's known as a *sai sin.* A monk ties the string around your wrist while chanting blessings. It can be red, white, yellow, or orange, depending on the tradition."

Riley leaned in, interested. "What does it mean?"

Mom smiled. "The thread symbolizes protection, against harm, illness, or negative energy. It also symbolizes connection, linking you to the Buddha, the Dharma, and the Sangha. And it serves as a reminder, to live mindfully, compassionately. People usually keep the string on until it naturally falls off. When it does, it's like the cycle of karma completing."

She set the string back down and added, "The kids and teenagers especially love them. Really, everyone wears them and doesn't take them off until they fall away. But they're actually an older tradition, something that goes back centuries. Which makes it a beautiful fit for the festival."

Riley rolled the thought around a moment, her chopsticks tapping lightly against her bowl. "So... it's not just decoration."

"Not at all," Mom said. "It's intention you carry with you. Some people will also ask about Aumé-Buddhism. All you need to tell them is this: Aumé is walking the Buddhist path while acknowledging the spirit. If they want more information, you can point them to aumé-buddhism.org."

Riley smiled. "That seems simple enough. And honest."

Sid finally looked up from demolishing his second basket. "So, basically, Riley gets to be the string lady."

Riley laughed. "I like that title."

Mom chuckled softly. "It's more than that, Sid. She'll be part of sharing something important. Each person who leaves with a string will carry a piece of what we believe."

Riley nodded thoughtfully, then grinned. "Cool. I can do that. Actually, I'm looking forward to it."

After lunch, Riley started stacking plates, but Mom stopped her with a smile. "No, no. Around here, the rule is: we cook, the boys clean."

That meant Sid and me. Of course.

Riley tried to sneak in a few dishes anyway, darting past me with the chopsticks bundle, but Mom wagged her finger. "Ah-ah. You're our guest."

So Sid and I scrubbed, wiped, and loaded the dishwasher while Riley "accidentally" dried a bowl or two when Mom wasn't looking. Once the last plate clattered into place and the dishwasher hummed to life, Mom declared the kitchen officially closed.

She and Sid carried their stack of library books off to the den, leaving the living room free.

Finally, Riley and I could get started on the real work of the day.

Music.

Chapter 44

Groov'n

The dumplings were amazing, like, stop-what-you're-doing-and-just-eat amazing, but I was glad we were done in the kitchen. I'd been waiting all day to get to the music. Finally, it was just me, Riley, two guitars, and the living room.

She set her case down, tuning up while I plugged into my little amp.

"Alright," she said, stretching her fingers, "dumpling time was fun, but this is the real work."

"Finally," I agreed. "I love dumplings, but they don't get us ready for Jeff on Wednesday."

She smirked. "Yeah, unless Jeff decides to open a food truck instead."

We both cracked up, but underneath it was the same thought: Jeff's glare from last night was still burned into our brains.

"Okay," Riley said, strumming a test chord. "If we can lock in, the others will follow."

I nodded. "Yeah. But we have to lead, not just survive." That's when Arthur's advice floated back into my head.

Slow it down. Listen first. Respect the story.

"Alright," I said, leaning forward. "Arthur always told me, 'Don't just play the notes. Listen until it lives in your bones. Slow it down until the story comes through.'"

Riley raised an eyebrow. "The story, huh? Okay, Mr. Storyteller. Where do we start?"

"Cross Road Blues. Johnson first. Then Cream."

She sat back, mock dramatic. "The bones and the big hair." I pulled up Robert Johnson's version on my phone. We listened in silence, Johnson's scratchy voice filling the room, his guitar buzzing like it was barely holding together.

Riley hugged her knees. "It's so bare. Like it's just him, daring the universe to knock him down."

"Exactly," I said. "That's the story."

She started strumming slow, humming first, then easing into the words. I joined in, picking the riff, careful not to rush. The first run? Disaster. I slipped on the turnaround, she lost her place, and we both collapsed into laughter.

"That was terrible," Riley said.

"Garbage," I agreed.

"Dumpster fire."

"Burning dumpster fire."

We sat there, grinning like idiots.

Then I said, "Arthur would say, one verse at a time. Respect the story."

She nodded. "One verse. No shortcuts."

We crawled through it again, slower. My fingers wanted to sprint ahead, but I forced them to stay put. Riley kept her voice steady, softer this time.

When we hit the turnaround clean, we both froze, eyes wide.

"That was it," she whispered.

"That was it," I echoed.

We did it again. And again. Each time, it stuck a little better.

"Okay," I said finally, flipping the distortion on. "Clapton's turn."

Her rhythm hardened, her voice stronger, and I leaned in with the riff. This time, it wasn't a fight. It was like we were pulling the same rope, hauling the song up the hill together. We collapsed after the chorus, sweaty and grinning. My fingers still buzzed.

"We're groov'n now," I said, trying to sound cooler than I felt.

Riley snorted. "Groov'n? Where did *that* come from?"

I shrugged, then grinned. "Records. You know, vinyl? Grooves in the wax? Arthur used to say the trick wasn't playing *fast,* it was staying in the groove. If you hop out of the groove, the needle skips, the whole song's wrecked."

Riley laughed so hard she nearly dropped her pick. "That's so old-school. But… okay, I like it."

Next was *The Thrill Is Gone.* Riley set the mood with those heavy minor chords, her strumming steady and sad. I bent the strings like B.B. King, letting the notes cry and wobble until they hurt.

"That's it," she said softly. "Make it ache."

Then we shifted into *Since I've Been Loving You.* She hit the chords harder, her voice rising, and I answered with long wails that made the amp buzz. For a minute, it almost felt like Zeppelin had borrowed our living room.

We both cracked up at the end, panting like we'd run laps. By the time we stumbled through *Hoochie Coochie Man* and *Smokestack Lightning,* it was nearly six. My fingers ached, her voice cracked, and my ears felt like cotton balls.

"That was brutal," Riley said, collapsing onto the rug.

"Yeah," I said, setting my guitar down carefully. "But not hopeless."

She sat up, smiling crookedly. "Not hopeless. I'll take it." That's when the knock came.

I dragged myself to the door and opened it. Jack stood there, soccer bag over his shoulder, hair still damp.

"Hey," he said. "Time to head out."

Riley groaned. "Already?"

"Already," Jack said firmly.

Mom appeared from the hallway holding a foil-wrapped bundle. "Here, take some dumplings home for your family.

Thank you for helping make them, and for agreeing to help with the booth."

Riley's cheeks flushed. "Thanks, Lily. Really."

Jack smirked. "Dumplings? Guess I picked the wrong night to be chauffeur."

Mom chuckled and pressed the bundle into Riley's hands. I walked her to the door. She gave me a quick smile, guitar slung over her shoulder, and was gone.

The living room went quiet, our guitars cooling in their stands. My fingers still buzzed, and Arthur's words echoed in my head.

Respect the story.

Chapter 45

Japan

"Hi Dad. How's the travel?"

I stretched out on my bed, the phone pressed to my ear. My guitar leaned against the desk, homework spread everywhere, but this call was way more interesting.

"On the way to Japan? Konichiwa!" I grinned. "Yeah, that's literally the only Japanese word I know. Don't test me."

I listened a moment, my smile fading. "Star is sick? Oh, that's not good. Like cancel-shows sick or just power-through sick?"

Dad must've said something about the schedule, because I sat up straighter. "Seven shows? In a baseball stadium? I didn't even know they played baseball in Japan!"

I laughed, then shook my head. "Yeah, yeah, I know, I should probably read more. But still, that's insane. Seven stadium shows in one run."

He said something about rehearsals and the setup. I pictured the stage being built, miles of cables snaking across a baseball diamond, soundchecks echoing in empty stands.

"That's wild. I mean, I thought Rock House was stressful, but at least no one's setting up pyrotechnics behind me. You've got fireworks, lights, giant video walls… and, oh yeah, 50,000 fans screaming."

I paused, picking up a pick off the nightstand and rolling it in my fingers. "So, are you nervous? Or is this, like, just another day at the office for you now?"

Dad's voice came through muffled, but I imagined him shrugging like he always did.

"Right," I said. "Do the work, don't overthink it. Chunk it out. Same stuff you tell me. Except my 'chunks' are middle school, kung fu, and learning how not to murder blues songs. Yours are, you know, keeping an entire stadium show from exploding. No pressure."

I lay back and stared at the ceiling. "Yeah, everything's good here. Two weeks till the Dragon Boat Festival. Pipa, I think I'm making progress. I guess we'll see in two weeks.

And the week after that is the end-of-season Rock House show, so… yeah. Super busy."

The door burst open and Sid charged in like he had radar for phone calls. "Is that Dad?!" He jumped on the bed, eyes wide, arms out.

I sighed, handed him the phone.

"Dad! Japan?!" Sid practically shouted into the receiver. "Bring me ninja stuff! And samurai swords! And cool things! Oh, and Bodhi has a girlfriend!"

"SID!" I lunged, trying to grab the phone back, but he was already giggling and rolling across the bed and out the door.

I gave up, sat back down, and picked up my guitar.

If Dad wanted to believe Sid's nonsense, fine. I slid into a riff, letting the strings buzz under my fingers, pretending my little brother hadn't just detonated my entire social life halfway across the Pacific.

And the old monk said, 'Or maybe she is your girlfriend, ha!"

Chapter 46

Two Weeks Fly by

The next two weeks flew by. School was a blur of math, history, and cafeteria noise. In Algebra, we moved on to quadratic equations, numbers turning into parabolas, parabolas turning into headaches. In Texas History, we started covering the Alamo. I kept thinking how cool it would be to actually go down to San Antonio later in the year, stand in front of the old mission, and see where it all happened.

The plants we'd seeded in gardening began to poke their little green heads through the soil. Nothing fancy yet, just sprouts, but it felt like proof that sometimes patience really does pay off.

The best part of every day, though, was lunch with Riley. Apples, carrots, crackers, nothing cafeteria hot-tray weirdness. Just us, laughing at Sid stories or arguing about whether Zeppelin or The Stones had better riffs.

(Answer: Zeppelin, but Riley pretends to disagree just to wind me up.)

Arthur kept me late after guitar more than once. And sometimes, instead of sending me home, he'd pull out the pipa and sit with me a while longer. "Slow it down," he'd remind me, tapping the table like a metronome. Sometimes he had me repeat a single phrase on the pipa for ten minutes straight. It was exhausting, but it got in my bones. His words followed me into everything else, kung fu drills, Lion Dance practice, even band rehearsal.

Speaking of kung fu, Sifu Huang pushed us harder each night in Lion Dance training. The lion head was heavier than it looked, the footwork sharper than I expected. Just when I thought our team was moving as one, he'd stop us and shout, "Again!" I swear I could feel my calves vibrating even when I was just sitting in class the next morning.

One Sunday, I got Dad on the phone. He was in Japan, the line crackly, his voice tired.

"Star's still sick?" I asked, stretching the phone cord across my room. "Man. Do you think the show will go on?"

There was a long pause, and I could picture him rubbing his forehead.

"Right," I said finally. "In this business, the show *always* goes on… except when it doesn't."

I laughed weakly. He probably had enough stress already without me piling on. We talked a little more, about stage setups and stadium crowds, and then he had to run.

That's when the Old Monk dropped by my brain. *"Time flies when you're having fun,"* he said, chuckling. *"Or when you're busy enough to forget you're tired."*

And just like that, we were staring down Dragon Boat weekend.

But first came Wednesday night.

Rock House.

Jeff had us back in the circle, instruments ready, eyes on him like he was a coach at halftime. He tapped the whiteboard with his marker.

"Crossroads. Thrill. Hoochie. Smokestack. Same pairings. This time, I want to believe you actually know what you're playing. Not just the notes, the *feel.*"

We started with *Cross Road Blues.* Riley caught my eye, and we both nodded. We'd worked this one, slowed it down, found the bones. The first verse held together, tight enough that Jeff actually stopped pacing for a second.

Then we shifted into Cream's *Crossroads.* Colt came in a little hot on the drums, Jett overcooked a bass run, and Riley's pick slipped mid-chorus. But it didn't collapse. We held on, rough edges and all.

Jeff lifted an eyebrow. "Better. You still sound like kids trying on grown-up shoes, but at least they fit this time."

We moved into *The Thrill Is Gone.* Riley's voice cracked on the first chorus, and she winced, but I bent a note long enough to cover the gap. She shot me a grateful look and pushed through.

"Okay," Jeff said when we finished. "That one had a pulse. Don't let it flatline halfway through."

By the time we reached *Hoochie Coochie Man,* we were sweating. Colt added a crash at the wrong moment, and Jeff whipped around.

"Colt! It's not called *'Cymbal Apocalypse.'* Less is more!"

The rest of us tried not to laugh while Colt shrugged sheepishly, twirling a stick.

We wrapped with *Smokestack Lightning*. Hypnotic. Messy. A little too loud. But together. For the first time, I felt like we weren't six kids pretending, we were almost, sort of, maybe becoming a band.

Jeff capped his marker and looked at us. "You're not there yet. But for the first time, I hear a band. Not just noise."

We all exhaled like we'd been holding our breath for two hours.

Outside afterward, we leaned against the wall, instruments still humming in our heads. Riley wiped sweat off her forehead with her sleeve.

"I think we survived," she said.

"Barely," I grinned. "But surviving counts."

She laughed. "Yeah. Surviving counts."

And with that, the countdown was over. Dragon Boat weekend had arrived.

Chapter 47
Training the Dragon

Mom drove us out to Twin Lake the next morning. Not the town, *the* lake. The real deal. I'd been out there before, but never like this. As soon as we pulled into the park near the hotels, it felt like we'd stepped into another world.

The shoreline was alive with color. Long, narrow dragon boats lined the water like a fleet of mythological creatures waiting to wake up. Their carved wooden heads, painted in reds and golds and greens, snarled toward the horizon, jaws open as if daring the lake itself to a fight. A couple of crews were already out paddling easy strokes, the steady *thunk* of their drums echoing over the water.

And this was just the day before the festival.

"Who knew so many people in North Texas were into dragon boat races?" I muttered as we parked.

Mom smiled, unbuckling Sid from the back seat. "You'd be surprised how many communities make this their big event of the year."

Sid practically leapt out of the car. "Come on, Bodhi! They're *right there!*" He grabbed my wrist and dragged me toward the docks. His little legs pumped like pistons, and he almost tripped twice, but nothing was going to stop him.

We weaved through tents, vendors, and clusters of people in matching shirts. Some were already stretching like they were prepping for the Olympics. Others were lounging on picnic blankets, sipping iced tea. The smell of grilled skewers and fried dumplings mixed with lake water and sunscreen.

Eventually we spotted a banner: **Twin Lakes Kung Fu**. That was us. A group of classmates and older students from Sifu Huang's studio had gathered near one of the boats, talking excitedly. And there was May, her long braid swinging as she waved.

"Hey, Bodhi!" she called. She was holding a small, decorated drum.

"You're the drummer?" I asked.

"Yup." She grinned. "Technically the caller, too. My job is to set the rhythm and yell at you all if you get sloppy." She gave the drum a test hit, *thump!*, and grinned wider. "I think I'm going to like this."

Sifu Huang gathered us together, his arms folded behind his back. "Today is training," he said simply. "Learn well. Tomorrow, you race."

A tall man in a windbreaker stepped forward. He had a whistle around his neck and a clipboard under his arm, looking every inch the coach.

"Name's Mr. Keller," he said, shaking a few hands. "I travel with these boats. Our team goes around the country, teaching groups like yours how to race. Some teams have their own equipment, the Twin Lakes Fire Department, for example. They've been the champs here seven years running."

Several of us groaned under our breath.

Mr. Keller smiled knowingly. "That doesn't mean they can't be beaten. New teams rise up all the time. But to have a shot, you need training, and you need heart."

He walked us down to the dock, where the dragon boat waited.

"Quick bit of history for you," he said, pausing by the carved dragon head at the bow. "Dragon boat racing began in China more than two thousand years ago. The story goes that it honors Qu Yuan, a poet who drowned himself in protest against corruption. Villagers raced out to save him, or at least recover his body, beating drums and splashing the water to scare away fish and evil spirits. That's why we race today, to honor courage, community, and tradition."

I glanced at the snarling dragon head. Suddenly it felt less like decoration and more like a guardian.

Mr. Keller blew his whistle. "Life jackets on!"

We wrestled into bright orange jackets that smelled faintly of plastic and lake water. Then, one by one, we climbed into the boat in pairs. The thing rocked underfoot, narrow and wobbly, but I found my seat next to Chan.

"Don't fall in," he whispered, grinning nervously.

"Not planning to," I muttered back.

Mr. Keller stood on the dock, hands cupped around his mouth. "First lesson, back paddle! Push yourselves away from the dock. Ready, stroke!"

We dug our paddles in backward. The boat jerked clumsily, half of us splashing more water onto each other than into the lake. Slowly, shakily, the boat drifted free.

"Good enough," Keller called. "Now, forward paddle. But listen to your drummer. She's your heartbeat. If you're not in sync, you don't move."

May sat tall at the bow, raised her sticks, and brought them down on the drum. *Thump! Thump! Thump!*

We tried to match her rhythm, paddles dipping and pulling as one. At first it was chaos, half the boat ahead, half behind, water sloshing everywhere. My paddle clacked into Chan's more than once.

"Together!" May shouted. *Thump! Thump! Thump!*

Slowly, the strokes evened out. The boat surged forward, gliding smoother, straighter.

"That's it!" Keller yelled. "That's dragon boating, twenty arms, one motion. Let the drum carry you."

The rhythm took hold. My shoulders burned, my palms stung, but for a moment I forgot the strain. All I heard was the drum, steady as a heartbeat, pulling us forward.

We practiced for nearly an hour, back paddling, racing starts, holding position. Keller barked commands, May kept us on beat, and gradually the boat started to feel less like a collection of kids and more like a single machine.

At one point, I remembered Mr. Daniels' boat safety class. Keep balanced, respect the water, trust your team. It all came back now, like the universe had lined it up on purpose.

When we finally pulled back to the dock, my arms were noodles, my shirt stuck to me with sweat. But my grin was huge.

Keller clapped his hands. "Not bad for your first session. Tomorrow, you'll face seasoned crews. But you've got fire, and that counts."

Sifu Huang's eyes swept over us. "Remember, it is not only about winning. It is about spirit, discipline, and respect. But if we paddle as one, " his eyes twinkled, "we *can* win."

We looked at each other, exhausted but buzzing. Twin Lakes Kung Fu was ready.

Tomorrow, race day!

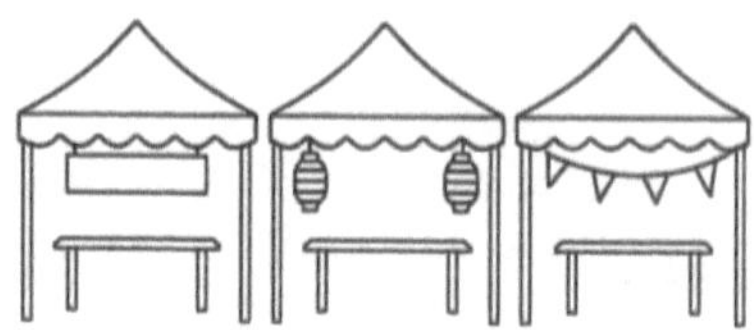

Chapter 48

Festival Morning

We got up early, so early even Sid didn't complain about breakfast. Mom had the car packed the night before with everything we'd need for the Aumé-Buddhism booth. Folding tables, banners, stacks of flyers, a cooler of water bottles, bags of rice crackers, even a couple of paper lanterns she insisted would "set the tone."

The volunteer parking area was at the far end of the park, which was both good (free) and bad (a long, long walk). Each trip felt like a mini-marathon. By the time we'd finished the first round, lugging tables, folding chairs, and a heavy box of brochures, I was already sweating through my T-shirt.

On our second trip back to the car, we spotted Riley. She was hopping out of Jack's old SUV, guitar case slung across her back. Jack gave us a quick wave before driving off. Riley saw us struggling with a stack of supply bins and ran over.

"Let me help," she said, grabbing the top box before I could argue.

"You're a lifesaver," I puffed. Sid was trying to balance a rolled-up banner on his shoulder like it was a medieval lance, weaving dangerously close to toppling.

The festival grounds were already buzzing even though it hadn't officially started. The air smelled like a mix of lake water and fried batter. A row of food tents stretched along one side, bursting with color. It wasn't just Chinese food either, Thai satay skewers sizzling on a grill, Vietnamese spring rolls wrapped in clear rice paper, Filipino halo-halo desserts in tall cups. People were chopping, stirring, stacking napkins, shouting instructions in three different languages all at once.

On the other side of the path, community booths were taking shape. Some had glossy sponsor signs, banks, car dealerships, local businesses. Others were cultural groups hanging fabric banners and setting out crafts. A Vietnamese lion costume rested on a rack, its sequined face glittering in the morning sun.

We hauled our supplies to the booth space Mom had reserved, a white canvas tent tucked between a calligraphy group and a booth selling bubble tea. Riley ducked inside and helped Mom unfold the tables. Sid, sweaty but proud, rolled out the banner across the grass.

It read in bright letters: **Aumé-Buddhism: Walking the Path, Embracing the Spirit.**

Mom fussed with the placement of the paper lanterns. "This corner feels a little bare," she murmured. Riley jumped in immediately, helping her adjust the decorations.

"I'll leave you two to handle the aesthetics," I said, wiping my forehead. "Sid and I are going to check out the boats."

Sid perked up instantly. He'd been buzzing since we got here, craning his neck for a glimpse of the dragon heads. He grabbed my hand and practically pulled me away from the booth.

That's when I realized the scope of it all. I'd pictured a few teams hanging around, maybe a couple of boats lined up on the lake. Instead, the grassy field along the shore was packed with team tents, rows and rows of them, each flying banners and flags like some kind of modern-day battlefield camp.

Everywhere I looked, teams were warming up. Some were stretching in perfect lines, counting out loud as they touched their toes and rotated their shoulders. Others were doing synchronized calisthenics, arms swinging and knees pumping in time. The Twin Lakes Fire Department team, undefeated champs, seven years in a row, were running drills across the grass, tight and silent, looking more like a squad of Navy SEALs than weekend paddlers.

The Old Monk chuckled, *"Is it any wonder that each year the firemen tame the fire-breathing dragon?"*

I blinked at another row of tents. These weren't just community groups. Corporate banners shouted at me in bold letters: **American Airlines. AT&T. Texas Instruments.** Each with matching shirts, water jugs, and gear lined up like it was a professional sporting event.

"Whoa," I muttered. "This is way bigger than I thought."

Sid's eyes were huge. "Do you think we can beat the firemen?"

I didn't answer right away. The firemen had muscles on top of muscles, and synchronized stretches that looked like they'd trained for this since kindergarten. But then I thought of May's drum, Sifu Huang's steady eyes, and our crew sweating through practice the day before.

"Maybe," I said finally. "If we paddle as one."

Sid nodded solemnly, like I'd just given him the secret password to victory.

We walked down toward the docks. The dragon boats gleamed in the morning sun, their heads fierce and proud, tails curling with painted scales. Crews were gathering in clusters, testing their paddles, laughing nervously. The lake stretched calm and wide, but you could feel the tension humming under the surface.

In just a couple hours the Dragons awake and the races begin!

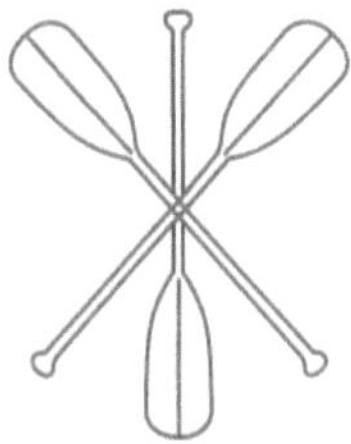

Chapter 49

Missing Paddlers

The races had begun. The announcer's voice boomed over the speakers, hyping up the crowd as the first heat's teams lined up at the starting line. Drums thundered across the water, and the air filled with cheering, whistles, and the sharp splash of paddles striking the lake in unison.

We weren't in that first heat. Twin Lakes Kung Fu was scheduled for the second. That gave us just enough time to get our act together, or so I thought.

I'd taken Sid back to the festival tents before the races started. He was supposed to hang around the booth with Mom, maybe hand out rice crackers and stay out of trouble. But the second he spotted the inflatable jump houses, his attention flew right out the window.

"Please, Bodhi!" he begged, practically bouncing in place. "Just one round! I'll be quick, I promise."

I sighed. Sid had one of those faces that made it nearly impossible to say no. "Fine. But stay where Mom can see you. I've got to get back to my team."

By the time I jogged back to the lake, the first heat was already underway. Boats sliced through the water, each crew paddling furiously in rhythm with their drummers. The crowd roared every time a team pulled ahead, and the energy was electric.

I spotted our team gathering near the dock and hurried over. But something was wrong.

Only fifteen people stood there, stretching, tightening life jackets, and fiddling nervously with their paddles. May, holding her drumsticks, was scanning the crowd like a hawk.

"Where's the rest?" I asked, dropping my bag at my feet.

She shook her head, her braid whipping behind her. "That's what I'm trying to figure out. We're supposed to have twenty paddlers. Ten rows of two, plus me on the drum and a steerer."

I counted quickly. "So... we're short five?"

"Yeah," she said grimly.

It didn't sound good, but I tried to reason it out. Yesterday, at training, we'd only had twelve paddlers. Mr. Keller hadn't made a big deal of it then, explaining that some people skipped training because they'd raced before and already knew what to do.

"Don't worry," Sifu had said. "They'll be there tomorrow."

Tomorrow was now today. And they weren't here.

My stomach sank. Yesterday Keller had also made it clear: dragon boats only worked if they were balanced. Every row had to be filled. If one side was heavier or lighter, the boat veered off course. Twenty paddlers moved as one. Fifteen couldn't pull it off.

Just then, Keller strode past us, clipboard in hand, his whistle bouncing against his chest. He was calling names, directing teams, checking life jackets. He glanced our way but didn't stop. Yet.

"Maybe they're just late?" I said, though it sounded weak even to me.

May tapped her drumsticks against her thigh. *Tap tap tap.* Her nervous habit. "Late doesn't cut it. If they don't show before we're called, we're out."

The crowd erupted as the first heat thundered toward the finish line. I caught glimpses of the firemen rowing in perfect sync, their arms pumping like machines. The announcer shouted over the cheers. "And the Fire Department takes it again! Seven years and counting!"

Great. As if we didn't already have enough pressure.

I scanned the crowd myself. Families waved flags. Food vendors called out specials. Kids darted around with sticky cotton candy fingers. But no sign of our missing paddlers.

"What happens if they don't come?" I asked.

"We forfeit," May said flatly. "Or… maybe Keller lets us borrow subs. Sometimes there are extras floating around."

"Forfeit?" The word hit me like a gut punch. After all our training? After sweating through practices, listening to May's drum until it echoed in my dreams? No way.

I clenched my paddle. "We're not forfeiting."

But the truth was, without those five, we might not have a choice.

The announcer's voice cut through the air again. "Heat Two, to the dock!"

That was us.

May's eyes went wide. "Oh no." We were out of time.

Chapter 50

The Magnificent Five

The announcer's voice boomed over the loudspeakers. "Heat Two, to the dock!"

May's face went pale. Fifteen paddlers stood ready. We needed twenty. Five missing seats stared back at us from the dragon boat, empty and accusing.

And then it happened.

From across the festival grounds, five figures came jogging toward us, paddles balanced on their shoulders like banners. For a moment, I thought my eyes were playing tricks on me. The crowd parted as they approached, just like in the old westerns my dad used to watch, The Magnificent Seven style, but this time there were only five.

"The cavalry," May breathed, her drumsticks clutched tight in her hand.

They were older, leaner, and more confident than most of us. Four men and one woman, all with the same calm, ready expressions. I recognized a couple of them from posters that hung in the Kung Fu school, students who had gone off to college.

"They're back?" I whispered.

"They came for this," said one of our green belts, awe in his voice.

The five strode up, each nodding at Sifu Huang before taking their places. One of them, a tall guy with short-cropped hair, clapped me on the shoulder as he passed. "You must be Bodhi. Don't worry. We've done this before."

Relief washed through me so fast it made me dizzy. Suddenly, our team was whole.

Mr. Keller, the Dragon Boat master, stopped his clipboard check when he saw them climb into the boat. His stern expression cracked into the faintest of grins. "Well, look at that. Twenty paddlers, right on time."

May tapped her sticks together. *Tap tap.* Not nervous this time, but eager. "Okay, team. Let's show them what Twin Lakes Kung Fu can do."

The announcer's voice rose again, calling the lineup for Heat Two. On the water, the firemen's boat glinted like polished steel, every rower snapping into position with military precision. Next to them, a corporate team in bright blue AT&T shirts looked loose and relaxed, chatting with each other like it was a company picnic. A community group in red vests stretched nervously.

And then there was us, finally twenty strong, finally complete.

We climbed into the dragon boat, the carved head bobbing slightly in the water as if nodding approval. I slid into my seat next to Chan, the paddle cool and solid in my hands. The five returning racers took their places like they'd never left, settling into rhythm with practiced ease.

May raised her sticks and looked down the length of the boat. "Twin Lakes!" she shouted.

"Kung Fu!" we answered, the call echoing back across the water.

The crowd loved it, cheering louder.

The five had come home, and with them, so had our confidence.

Chapter 51

First Race

We didn't have much time for introductions beyond a couple of quick high-fives and a breathless, *"Glad you're here."* The announcer was already booming over the speakers, calling our heat to the dock.

May jogged to the front of the boat, drumsticks tucked under her arm. She settled into the drummer's seat, the carved dragon head jutting out just in front of her, its teeth bared toward the lake. Mr. Keller positioned himself at the rear, paddle in hand, ready to steer us straight. Ten rows of two stretched out in between, each seat filled now, twenty paddlers, shoulder to shoulder, ready to move.

I slid into my place beside Chan. The wooden seat felt narrow, the paddle heavy in my grip. My heart was already pounding, though the race hadn't even started.

The announcer's voice carried across the water. "Heat Two: on the inside lane, Twin Lakes Police Department! Next to them, American Airlines! In the middle, Twin Lakes Kung Fu! Lane four, Muay Thai Dallas! And on the outside, Golden Dragon Restaurant!"

The crowd roared. Sid's voice rose above them all: "GO BODHI!"

I grinned in spite of my nerves.

"Ready your paddles!" Keller barked.

May raised her sticks high above her head. The world seemed to hold its breath.

The starting horn blared.

THUMP! THUMP! THUMP!

May's drum thundered, and our paddles hit the water as one. The boat lurched forward, slicing into the lake.

The first few strokes were chaos, splashing water, paddles clattering, but then the rhythm locked in. May's beat was steady, Keller's voice sharp and clear.

"Drive! Drive! Drive!"

The water foamed at our sides as twenty paddles rose and fell in unison. Spray hit my face, cool and stinging. My arms already burned, but I forced the paddle deeper, pulled harder, kept my eyes on the back of the head in front of me. Don't think, just move.

On our left, American Airlines surged ahead early, their blue shirts flashing in the sun. But by the halfway mark, they started to wobble, strokes uneven, water splashing too high. On our right, the Golden Dragon team fought to keep their boat straight, their steerer shouting as they drifted sideways.

That left three boats in the lead: us, Muay Thai, and the Police.

The Muay Thai team grunted with each stroke, fierce and fast. But the Police, oh man. They were a machine. Perfect timing, not a splash wasted. Their boat glided like it was on rails, pulling ahead with every beat.

"Power! Power! Power!" May shouted, slamming the drum.

We answered. Muscles screamed, lungs burned, but we kept driving. The lake blurred into sunlight and spray. For a moment, I thought we might catch them.

But the Police held their lead.

The horn blasted again, finish line.

We surged past in second place, a full boat length behind the Police but just ahead of Muay Thai.

"Twin Lakes Police, first place! Twin Lakes Kung Fu, second! Muay Thai Dallas, third!" the announcer called.

The crowd erupted, and even though we hadn't won, I couldn't help grinning. We'd done it, we'd raced, and we hadn't sunk.

We coasted to the dock, paddles dripping, chests heaving. Keller barked instructions as we steadied the boat against the rail. My legs wobbled when I climbed out, every muscle jelly, but Sid's cheer from the sidelines made me stand a little taller.

There wasn't time to celebrate.

Chapter 52
Forms

"Forms team, you're up!" Sifu Huang's voice cut through the noise.

I blinked. "Now?!"

"Now!" he said firmly.

We dropped paddles, shook out our arms, and sprinted across the field. Past the sponsor tents, past the food stalls, past the inflatable dragon arch that marked the main stage. From lake to stage was probably just short of a quarter mile.

Behind the stage, we quickly changed into our demonstration uniforms. Damp racing shirts and life jackets were tossed aside, replaced with crisp Kung Fu jackets and sashes. The switch alone helped me focus, out of the boat, into the art.

When we filed onto the stage, the boards under our feet felt steady, nothing like the rocking dragon boat. The emcee gave a short welcome, then stepped back. The crowd settled, phones came up, voices dropped. This wasn't a cheer-for-points thing. It was sharing.

My chest was still heaving from the race, but the adrenaline carried me.

Sifu Huang stood offstage, arms folded, watching.

"Begin!" he called.

We moved.

First up were the green and orange belts, my group. We stepped forward in formation. Our movements were precise, steady, and clear. Front kicks, straight punches, horse stances rooted into the stage. Nothing flashy, but disciplined. This was the foundation, the building blocks.

When our set finished, we bowed and stepped back. The purple and brown belts flowed in. Their routines were sharper, faster, their strikes snapping louder. Some carried weapons, long staffs spinning in controlled arcs, swords flashing briefly in the sunlight. They moved with a confidence I couldn't wait to earn.

And then came the black belts. The stage felt like it shifted under their presence. Their forms were fluid yet powerful, acrobatics threaded into their movements. One leapt into a twisting kick that seemed to hang in the air. Another spun twin broadswords with such precision the blades seemed to sing. The finale was Monkey Form, agile, unpredictable, part martial art and part theater. The black belt crouched low, bounding, twisting, scratching, then exploding into sudden strikes that made the younger kids gasp.

The audience stayed mostly quiet, respectful. A few murmurs of appreciation rippled here and there when a staff cracked against the stage with perfect timing, or when a sword cut the air just so. Parents lifted phones to film, but mostly people just watched. It wasn't about applause. It was about honoring the art.

I stood at the back with my team, catching my breath, feeling both proud of what we'd shown and humbled by what was still ahead of us.

This was Kung Fu not as a competition, but as a culture, passed from teacher to student, and shared here so the whole community could see its spirit.

By the final bow, my arms still ached from the race, but I felt lighter. We had done our part, one layer in the ladder of tradition.

Race one was over; and Twin Lakes Kung Fu had represented well. But the day was just beginning.

Chapter 53
Lion Dance

Still humming from the morning's race and forms, I thought I would check-in with how Mom, Riley, and Sid were doing at the Aumé- Buddhism booth. They were swamped, people spilling out in front of the tent, kids holding up their wrists proudly to show off their new protection strings. Teens were laughing, parents smiling, even a few grandparents stopping by to ask questions. Sid was working hard, too, running cards and strings back and forth like it was his personal mission.

The booth was hopping. Meiling was there as well. TI thanked her for the Pipa, and she said she looked forward to seeing me play later in the show.

Riley and I managed to sneak away for a quick bite at a food truck parked nearby. The smell of fried dumplings pulled us in like a magnet. We found a shady spot under a tree, paper trays in hand.

"So," Riley asked, blowing on her dumpling before biting in, "how was the first race?"

I told her about the start, how we fought our way into rhythm, how the Police team seemed like a machine. Then I described the mad sprint from the dock to the stage, changing into our uniforms, and performing the forms. Riley listened, nodding between bites.

"Sounds exhausting," she said with a grin.

"Pretty much," I admitted. "But also awesome."

We barely had time to eat half a dumpling each before I spotted Sifu Huang near the stage, waving his arms like he was calling in reinforcements.

"Lion Dance!" I said, hopping up.

Riley stuffed the rest of her dumpling in her mouth and ran with me.

Behind the stage, it was chaos. Students were already pulling on their uniforms, cymbals were clashing in warm-up, and three lion heads waited on the ground, their bright colors gleaming in the sun, red and gold, green and white, and yellow trimmed with black.

"Bodhi, May, you're on yellow!" Sifu barked.

I froze for half a second, then grabbed the heavy lion head while May ducked inside to take the tail. My heart was still racing from the boat and the forms, but this was different. This was pure adrenaline.

We crouched into position as the drum thundered out front, steady and strong. The cymbals followed, sharp and bright. Someone shouted, "Go!" and we bounded out from behind the stage.

The crowd parted with gasps as three lions leapt into the open space.

The red lion charged first, snapping its head up and down, eyes blinking, mouth clapping open and shut. The green lion darted after it, playful and teasing, weaving through the crowd. Then May and I surged forward with the yellow lion, bounding in time with the drumbeat. The lion's head was heavy, hot, and awkward, but when I tilted it and blinked the eyes, the crowd responded like it was alive.

We circled, three lions moving in rhythm, tails swaying, paws stamping the ground in unison. The drummers picked up speed, the cymbals crashing harder and harder until the sound shook in my chest.

Red leapt onto a raised platform, balancing proudly. Green followed, twisting around to challenge it. Then May gave me the signal from inside the tail, our turn. I bent low, then sprang up, jerking the head high as we bounded onto our own platform. The crowd gasped and clapped as we teetered for a second before settling steady.

"Keep it alive," I muttered, working the lion's mouth open and shut, nodding the head proudly. May swished the tail behind me with perfect timing.

The three lions squared off, mock fighting, leaping and rolling across the stage area. Kids squealed, adults laughed, and cameras flashed. I lost track of time completely, my whole world shrank down to the drumbeat, May's signals behind me, and the heavy lion head bobbing in my hands.

At the finale, all three lions crouched low, then reared back together, eyes wide and mouths gaping. The drums thundered one last roll, cymbals crashed, and we froze in a fierce, triumphant pose.

The crowd erupted in applause, warm, respectful, loud enough to make my chest hum even after we stepped back.

We ducked out of the lion, drenched in sweat, hair plastered to our foreheads. May grinned at me, still breathless.

"That," she said, "was worth every bruise from practice."

I couldn't help smiling back. She was right.

Chapter 54
The Parade

As soon as the Lion Dance performance ended and the crowd's applause faded into chatter, Sifu Huang gathered us quickly behind the stage. "No resting yet," he said, voice firm but not unkind. "Parade formation. The whole festival must see the lions today."

The word *parade* hit me harder than the race or the forms. The festival grounds wrapped around Twin Lake in a huge loop, easily half a mile, maybe more. Marching the whole way in costume, under the October Texas sun, sounded like slow torture.

But there was no saying no.

The three lion costumes were lined up, along with drummers and cymbal players who would pound out rhythm along the route. Around us, other groups assembled too, the Thai dancers in their gleaming silk skirts, golden crowns perched carefully on their heads; an Indonesian troupe with tall feathered headdresses; martial artists from other schools, each carrying banners with Chinese characters painted in bold red strokes. At the front were local leaders, community organizers, and the festival president in a broad-brimmed hat, already fanning himself with the event program.

It was going to be a show.

I crouched back under the yellow lion head, May tugging the tail into place behind me. Sweat had already started dripping into my eyes, and we hadn't even moved yet.

"Ready?" I whispered.

"Not even close," she said, though her laugh gave me courage.

The drums started.

BOOM. BOOM. BOOM.

We surged forward with the parade.

The lions bounded in time with the drums, weaving playfully as the parade wound past the first stretch of booths. The red lion snapped its head at a row of kids holding bubble tea, making them squeal and laugh. The green lion crouched low, sniffing around a taco stand before springing back up with exaggerated surprise, earning a round of applause from the booth workers.

I tried to keep our yellow lion lively, tilting the head side to side, blinking the eyes, snapping the mouth. Every time I jerked the head too hard, sweat ran down my back, soaking my uniform. Inside the lion, the air felt heavy, like a sauna that followed me wherever I went.

"This is worse than sparring drills," I muttered.

"Keep moving!" May urged from the tail. "If you slow down, it looks weird!"

So I kept moving.

The parade wound around the lake, past rows of vendor tents. The smells were almost unbearable, dumplings steaming, skewers sizzling, sweet fried dough dusted with sugar. Every breath carried a new temptation. My stomach growled, reminding me we never actually finished our dumplings.

The Thai dancers moved gracefully behind us, somehow looking cool and serene despite their heavy costumes. Their hands curled into intricate shapes with each step, their feet tapping softly on the hot pavement. Behind them, the Indonesian drummers pounded on tall barrel drums, their rhythms twining with our lion beats in a chaotic but joyful collision.

Crowds lined the path, clapping, waving, snapping pictures. Some reached out to touch the lions for luck. Each time, I tried to dip the head respectfully, blinking the eyes like a bow.

Halfway around, the sun really started to bite. My arms trembled from holding the lion's head steady, my shoulders burned, and every breath inside the costume was like breathing through a hot towel.

"I can't believe firemen do this in full gear," I muttered.

"Stop whining," May shot back, though I could hear the exhaustion in her voice too.

We pressed on.

The parade turned down a shaded stretch lined with trees, and I nearly cried with relief. A breeze drifted off the lake, cool and sweet, drying the sweat on my face just enough to keep me going. Kids darted along the sidelines, running ahead to catch another glimpse of the lions. Somewhere in the crowd, I heard Sid's unmistakable cheer: "That's my brother! That's him in the yellow lion!"

I grinned inside the costume, even if no one could see it.

The parade circled past the main sponsor tents, American Airlines, AT&T, TI, all with their employees waving, some in matching T-shirts, some fanning themselves with paper fans. The police team stood proudly outside their tent, holding their paddles like trophies. One of them gave me a nod as we passed, and I blinked the lion's eyes back in salute.

Finally, after what felt like forever, we looped back toward the festival stage. The drummers rolled into a final booming crescendo. All three lions crouched low, then leapt high together, tails snapping behind them. The cymbals clashed one last time, ringing over the crowd.

And then it was over.

We ducked out of the lion costumes, drenched, hair plastered to our foreheads, uniforms sticking to us. My arms felt like wet noodles, my back ached, and I was sure I smelled like a gym bag left in the sun.

But the smiles on the crowd, the waves from kids, the nods from elders along the parade route, it made the heat and sweat worth it.

May flopped down onto the grass beside me, fanning herself with one of the lion tails. "Next year," she said, "we get the short parade."

"Next year," I agreed, though I wasn't sure I meant it.

The Old Monk's voice slipped into my head, calm and amused: *"Some dragons breathe fire. Others simply cook you slowly under the sun."*

I laughed to myself. He wasn't wrong.

Chapter 55

The Second Race

We were still sweating inside the lion costumes when the announcer's voice thundered across the lake:

"Heat Four, paddlers to your boats!"

May and I yanked off the lion head and tail, stuffing them quickly into the big canvas bags to haul back to the cars later. No time to rest. No time to breathe.

"Go! Go!" Sifu Huang shouted.

I spotted Mom, Sid, and Riley near the Aumé booth as I sprinted back toward the docks. I waved quickly. Sid tried to chase after me, but Mom snagged his arm before he could dart into the crowd. Riley grinned, raising a dumpling like a toast before the three of them faded behind me.

The docks were chaos. Teams lined up in clusters, life jackets snapping shut, paddles stacked in neat rows. We had to squeeze through lines of waiting crews just to reach our boat. My legs still felt like noodles from the parade, and my lungs burned like I'd been sprinting laps in the Texas sun all day, which I basically had.

Keller barked instructions as we clambered aboard. "Straps tight! Feet locked in! Listen for May!"

We shoved off.

The lake glittered painfully bright in the afternoon sun. Across from us, the other boats lined up: the Twin Lakes Fire Department in their matching shirts, solid as a wall of stone; American Airlines, calm and loose, stretching like cats; and AT&T, their paddles gleaming with fresh sponsor logos.

"Heat Four, on my signal!" Keller called.

I gripped my paddle tighter, sweat stinging my eyes. My arms trembled from holding the lion head earlier. I wasn't sure how much more I had in me, but there was no backing out now.

The horn blared.

BOOM! BOOM! BOOM!

May's drum thundered, and we lunged forward. Paddles bit into the water, pulling us in rhythm. Spray splashed up, cooling my face for half a second before the sun dried it again.

"Drive! Drive! Drive!" Keller yelled from the back.

We drove.

For the first fifty meters, we held strong, even edging ahead of AT&T. But then the Fire Department surged. Their strokes were pure power, their timing perfect, like a machine built for this moment. They glided ahead.

American Airlines pressed next, slipping past us on the other side. I tried to push harder, but my lungs were already screaming, every stroke a war. I could feel the whole boat sagging under the weight of exhaustion. All the running, the forms, the lion dance, it was catching up to us now.

By the halfway mark, it was clear: this wasn't our heat to win. The Firemen held first, American Airlines second, and we were locked in a desperate battle with AT&T just to avoid last.

"Together!" May roared, pounding the drum.

We dug in, fighting for every inch. The lake churned under us, white foam splashing up as paddles slammed harder, faster. At the last moment, we surged just ahead of AT&T.

The horn blared. Finish.

"Firemen first, American Airlines second, Twin Lakes Kung Fu third, AT&T fourth!" the announcer called.

Cheers rolled over the lake, but all I could do was drop my paddle across my lap and suck in air like I'd never breathe again. My arms shook uncontrollably. My whole shirt clung to me, soaked with sweat and lake spray.

We had placed third. Not great. Not terrible.

But it wasn't over yet.

Back on shore, we learned how the scoring worked. The festival used a point-and-time system: each team's finish place and race times were added up to determine who made the final heats. The winners weren't just the fastest in one race, they had to prove consistency across all of them.

That meant we still had a chance at another shot.

The wait was brutal. Other heats came and went. I tried sitting under a tree in the shade, but my legs cramped if I stopped moving. Vendors shouted out specials, ice cream, lemonade, fried rice, but I didn't dare eat more than a sip of water. My stomach was too tight with nerves.

Finally, after what felt like forever, the announcer returned to the mic.

"The standings are posted! For the finals: the Fire Department and Police Department will meet in Race One for first and second place."

The crowd erupted. Everyone expected that showdown, it was the clash of titans, the two local powerhouses with their own boats and year-round training.

"And for the third-place final: Twin Lakes Kung Fu, American Airlines, and two community teams, Golden Dragon Restaurant and Team Core!"

I clenched my fists, relief surging through me. We were still alive.

"Race Two paddlers, report to the dock in twenty minutes!"

That was us.

We had one last shot to prove ourselves, one last chance to fight for a medal.

I looked around at my teammates, sweaty, tired, but standing straighter now. Even May's drumsticks tapped with renewed energy.

"Third place," I muttered to myself. "Let's go get it."

The old monk said, "The river does not ask if it flows first, second, or third. It only asks, do you paddle?"

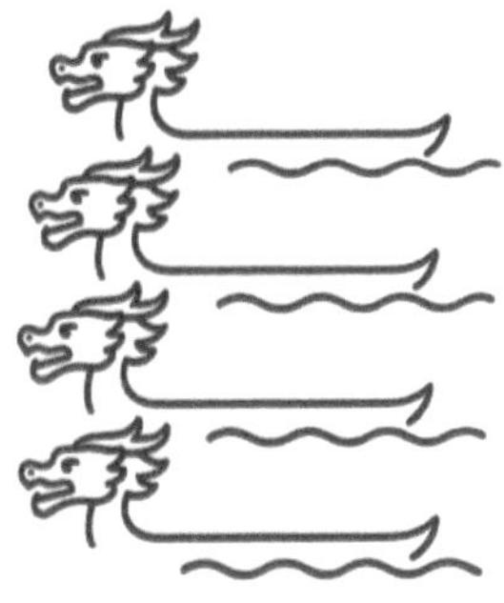

Chapter 56

Four Dragons

It had already been the longest.. Two Dragon Boat races, Kung Fu forms on stage, a full Lion Dance performance, and then the parade around the festival grounds in the blazing Texas sun. By late afternoon, my uniform was stiff with dried sweat, my arms ached like I'd been wrestling trees, and my throat was raw from shouting calls with the team.

And still, it wasn't over.

The final race loomed, our last shot at a medal. But my mind kept flicking back to the stage on the other side of the festival grounds, where the schedule was ticking closer and closer to my slot for the Pipa performance. I was supposed to be ready to play in front of thousands of people, parents, teachers, strangers, everyone. Instead, I was gripping a paddle, heart hammering, sweat dripping into my eyes.

The firemen and the police had already finished their showdown, just like everyone expected. Firemen first. Police second. Titans battling for bragging rights.

Now it was our turn, Race Two, the fight for third place. Twin Lakes Kung Fu versus American Airlines, Golden Dragon Restaurant, and Team Coppell Rec Center.

"Paddlers to the dock!" the announcer called.

I swallowed hard. This was it.

As we strapped in, I could hear faint music from the stage drifting across the water. A performance ending. Applause rising. My stomach twisted. *They're close. They're almost at me.*

But a race is only five minutes. I told myself I could do both. Paddle like mad, win third, sprint off the dock, and make it to the stage in time. Easy. Right?

"Paddles ready!" Keller barked from the back.

May raised her drumsticks. Her face was fierce, determined. She wasn't thinking about stages or Pipas or anything else. Just the race. I wished I could be her for five minutes.

The horn blasted.

We shoved off, paddles biting into the lake with a splash. The boat lunged forward, water spraying cold against my face.

"Drive! Drive! Drive!" May roared, pounding the drum in a rhythm that rattled my bones.

We drove.

American Airlines matched us stroke for stroke. Their paddles slapped the water like clockwork, their boat riding our wake. Golden Dragon fell back early, their timing messy, and Coppell Rec struggled just to stay straight. It was down to us and the Airline crew.

The crowd onshore blurred, a wall of sound, shouts, cheers, cymbals clashing from somewhere. My arms burned, my shoulders felt like fire, but I refused to let go of the rhythm. Stroke. Stroke. Stroke.

Halfway across, they pulled even with us. I clenched my teeth, forcing the paddle deeper, water churning around us in froth. May's drumbeat grew frantic, faster and faster, willing us to match her.

"Together!" she screamed.

We answered, twenty paddles slamming the water in unison. Our boat surged, inch by inch, ahead of the Airlines team.

The finish line buoys rushed closer. The roar of the crowd grew. My lungs begged for air, my arms begged for mercy. But I gave neither.

One last push.

The horn blared.

We shot across first in our heat, third place overall. Bronze for Twin Lakes Kung Fu.

The team erupted, paddles raised, shouts echoing across the lake. Relief and pride flooded me. We had done it. We had beaten the odds.

But even in that rush of triumph, I heard it.

My name.

"Bodhi Dharma!" A voice boomed faintly over the festival speakers. "Please come to the stage for the next performance, Bodhi Dharma!"

My stomach dropped through the floor of the boat.

I wasn't just needed anymore. I was late!

Chapter 57

Smaller than the Tide

The Thai dancers spun in a final flourish, silk sleeves trailing like fire. The drums cut off with a crash, and the crowd erupted, applause echoing across the lakefront.

The woman running the stage, in her red cheongsam and headset mic, stepped forward, smiling wide. "And now, for something very special. Please welcome a young man you're going to hear about for years to come. On pipa... Bodhi Dharma!"

The audience hushed. Heads turned toward the wings.

Nothing.

The woman tried again. Louder this time. "Bodhi Dharma!"

No Bodhi. Just empty space and the faint buzz of the mic.

A ripple of murmurs spread through the crowd. The woman frowned, clearly stalling. "Perhaps he is... preparing backstage. One last call for Bodhi Dharma!"

Still nothing.

Her smile wavered. She raised her hand toward the sound booth, clearly ready to cut the set. "Well, it seems we may have to, "

"Wait!"

A voice rang out, young and clear. Riley stepped into the light, guitar case slung over her shoulder. She looked so small against the vastness of the stage, the crowd stretching into darkness, faces blinking back at her. She bent quickly, unlatched her case, and pulled out her battered acoustic guitar.

"Hey there," she said into the mic, her voice shaky but loud enough to carry. "I'm here for Bodhi. He's... well, he's in the Dragon Boat finals, and he's not here yet. So... I'd like to share a song."

The woman in red stepped forward, her face tightening. "I'm sorry, but, "

But Riley had already slipped the strap over her shoulder and strummed one soft chord. The mic caught it, the sound blossoming out across the speakers. A few people in the audience chuckled nervously, but most just turned to the woman onstage. She hesitated, then the strangest thing happened: the audience started clapping softly, encouraging. Someone called out, "Let her play!" Another voice: "Give her a chance!"

The woman frowned, but the crowd had spoken. With a little shake of her head, she backed into the wings.

Riley swallowed hard, adjusted her guitar, and stepped closer to the mic. "This is a song I've been working on. A while back, I was walking alone on the beach in Oregon, down to this cove at the bottom of a cliff. The ocean was huge, endless. I felt so small I wondered if I even mattered. This is what came out of that moment. I hope you'll listen."

She strummed again, a gentler chord, and began to sing.

"Its called, '**Smaller Than the Tide**"

I was standing by the water
Where the cliffs rise high and steep,
Waves were rolling in forever,
Secrets only oceans keep.

And I wondered if I mattered,
Or if I could just fade away.
But the tide kept on returning,
Like it had something to say.

Her voice was trembling, but pure. In the front rows, a little girl tugged at her mother's sleeve, whispering, "She sounds pretty." The mother nodded, eyes already glassy.

By the time Riley reached the chorus, the crowd had gone completely silent.

I'm smaller than the tide,
But I'm still here, I'm alive.
Every wave that knocks me down
Teaches me how to survive.
I'm smaller than the tide,
But I'm stronger than the fear.
If the ocean sings forever,
Then I know I'm meant to be here.

Somewhere halfway back, a man in a baseball cap lowered his phone mid-text and just listened.

An older couple clasped hands. A group of high schoolers stopped their chatter and swayed unconsciously to the rhythm. Riley wasn't flashy. She wasn't perfect. But she was real.

Her voice wavered again on the second verse, but instead of breaking, it cracked with emotion. That only made it stronger.

Sometimes life can feel like thunder,
Storms that shake you to the bone.

But the stars still burn above us,
Even when we feel alone.

So I'll listen to the silence,
And the song beneath the spray,
'Cause the ocean's voice reminds me,
That the dark won't wash away.

She closed her eyes as she sang, her fingers steady on the strings. In the crowd, a teenage boy wiped his eyes quickly before anyone saw. The song wasn't just hers anymore, it was theirs, too.

When Riley hit the bridge, the air seemed to shift. People leaned forward, phones lifted now not to distract but to capture the moment.

The waves don't ask permission,
They just crash and then they rise.
But I've got my own rhythm,
Like the fire in the skies.

Her final chorus rose like a tide. Stronger, braver, filled with everything she had.

I'm smaller than the tide,
But I'm still here, I'm alive.
Every wave that knocks me down
Teaches me how to survive.
I'm smaller than the tide,

But I'm stronger than the fear.
If the ocean sings forever…
Then I know I'm meant to be here.

She let the last chord ring, her head bowed, eyes closed. The silence afterward stretched impossibly long, and then the dam broke.

Applause roared up like a wave crashing against the cliffs. Whistling, stomping, clapping that shook the air. People leapt to their feet, cheering for the girl with the guitar who had walked into their evening and sung straight from her heart.

Riley opened her eyes, stunned. For a second she looked like she might cry. Then she smiled, a smile so wide and unguarded that the whole lakefront seemed to glow.

And out there, still running, Bodhi wasn't even close yet.

Chapter 58
The Stage

I ran.

The dock boards rattled under my soaked shoes, the festival grounds a blur of color and sound. My chest heaved, my legs wobbled, but I couldn't stop. The crowd was everywhere, kids darting with balloon animals, parents balancing trays of food, music thundering from the stage ahead.

And then I heard it.

Riley's voice.

High, clear, raw in a way that made the air itself hold still. She was singing her beach song, the one she told me about, when the ocean had made her feel small and powerful at the same time. The crowd was silent, listening, caught in her words. Even the food vendors had stopped shouting.

I stumbled to a halt for half a second, just to hear. My throat tightened. She had done this, for me.

The song rose, quivered, and finally faded into the lake breeze. Applause swelled, rolling across the festival grounds like a wave.

And then something new began.

Stomp. Stomp. Clap.
Stomp. Stomp. Clap.

The sound of a thousand feet and hands echoing together, steady, unstoppable. It was Queen's rhythm, the one from *We Will Rock You*. I'd heard it at baseball games, basketball games, even in gym class when someone smacked two textbooks together just to imitate it. And now, here it was, alive, shaking the grass under my feet.

Stomp. Stomp. Clap.
Stomp. Stomp. Clap.

The crowd was calling me in.

I pushed harder, weaving through the crush of people, sweat flying from my face. My stomach lurched like I might collapse, but I kept going.

At the edge of the stage, Sid popped out of nowhere, holding up a water bottle like he was in a marathon pit crew. "Go, Bodhi!" he yelled.

I grabbed it without breaking stride, chugged half of it, and felt the cold water burn down my throat. The rest splashed across my face, cooling me just enough to keep me upright. I tossed the empty bottle back, and Sid caught it like a pro.

Then I was climbing the stage steps, legs trembling, the stomp-clap rhythm pounding louder with every second.

Riley was waiting. She looked like she'd just run her own marathon, her hair damp with sweat, her cheeks flushed, but her smile steady. When I reached her, she squeezed my hand, quick, fierce, enough to say *you made it, now finish this.*

Someone, I didn't even see who, slipped the pipa strap over my shoulder. The instrument rested against my chest, warm wood against my still-heaving ribs. I adjusted the strap, fingers brushing the strings, heart pounding so hard it felt like the drumline was inside me.

The mic loomed ahead, silver and still, waiting.

I took one shaky step forward.

And then another.

The crowd stomped and clapped in rhythm, louder, louder, until it was impossible to tell if it was in the ground, the sky, or just my own head.

I gripped the pipa's neck tight, lifted my eyes, and approached the microphone.

The stomp-clap faded into a restless hush as I stepped up to the microphone. The pipa was heavy against my chest, its smooth wood warm from the late-day sun. My fingers hovered over the strings, itching to play, but for a moment I just looked.

Out over the crowd, faces blurred into a sea of color, festival banners waving, phones raised, paper lanterns bobbing in the breeze. And then, among the thousands, I began to spot them.

Mom stood near the front, hands clasped together, eyes bright and steady on me. Beside her, my breath caught, Dad. He must have flown straight in, because he still wore his black travel jacket, hair wild from the wind. He grinned at me and gave a huge thumbs-up, the kind that used to make me laugh when I was little. I laughed now, and it settled my nerves.

Sid was bouncing up and down next to them, waving his arms like he was trying to land an airplane. I gave him a little nod, and he pumped his fists like we'd already won. Riley slipped into place beside my family, her smile quiet but fierce. She'd carried this moment for me, and now she was handing it back.

Further out, I saw more, Sifu Huang and the Kung Fu team, still in their uniforms, standing together like a proud wall. And Arthur, Arthur was here too, leaning casually against a tent pole, arms crossed, but his eyes sharp on me. When he noticed I'd spotted him, he tipped his chin as if to say, *You know what to do, kid.*

My throat felt tight. The pipa strap pulled heavier on my shoulder. I leaned into the mic, heart pounding.

"First… thank you," I said, my voice rough but steady. "Thank you to all of you for waiting for me, and thank you to Riley, Rile, I heard you. You sounded beautiful, as always."

Riley ducked her head, cheeks flushing. The crowd murmured softly, warm with appreciation.

I took a breath, letting the silence stretch, then went on.

"I would like to thank my mother's friend, Meiling. Her father played this pipa his whole life. And now… it is my honor to play it for all of you."

I let the words hang there, resting my hand gently on the strings. The instrument seemed to hum under my fingers, as if it were alive, waiting, carrying all the weight of history, of family, of music that had come before.

The crowd leaned forward, quiet, expectant.

I lowered my eyes, found my breath, and prepared to play.

Chapter 59

The Pipa Sings

I closed my eyes, let the mic fade away, and touched the first string.

The pipa answered.

Notes tumbled out like sparks from flint, sharp, fast, urgent. "Ambush from Ten Sides." The battle piece. My fingers rolled the tremolo until it sounded like galloping hooves, like steel clashing against steel. The strings cried out in flurries and hammered rhythms, the story of warriors charging across fields that had turned to chaos.

The crowd leaned forward. No one moved. Even the kids in the bouncy house stopped mid-jump to stare.

I pushed deeper, the notes boiling over, and then, just when it seemed like the clash of armies would never end, I slowed. The tremolo softened, stretched, bent. The battlefield melted into something else.

Blues.

I slid into a riff, slow and aching, the kind Arthur had told me to live inside. The notes bent and moaned like a voice calling out across a river. I thought of B.B. King, of the pain in *The Thrill Is Gone,* and I let it leak out through my fingers. It wasn't Chinese or American, not ancient or modern. It was just human.

The crowd swayed. People in the front row closed their eyes, hands pressed to their hearts. Somewhere near the side, I saw Riley's lips part, just barely, as though she could feel the story unfolding inside the notes.

And then, without even thinking, I struck harder. The blues phrase twisted, stretched, and erupted into something louder, faster, wilder.

Rock.

The tremolo became a scream. My hand raked the strings in a fury, like Jimmy Page tearing through *Since I've Been Loving You.* The stomp-clap rhythm the crowd had carried earlier returned on its own, building under me, driving me higher.

I didn't fight it. I leaned into the storm.

The pipa wailed, then whispered, then roared again. For three and a half minutes the world dissolved into sound: East and West, past and present, battle and heartbreak and triumph all packed into one instrument, one song, one kid who had no business pulling it off but did anyway.

When I hit the final chord, it rang like a bell. A single, shimmering note that refused to fade. Silence. And then, thunder.

The crowd erupted, cheers rolling over the lake, claps and stomps shaking the grass underfoot. Flags waved, phones shot up, kids jumped on shoulders just to see. For one dizzying moment, I felt bigger than myself. Not famous, not perfect, just... connected. To the pipa. To Riley. To my family. To everyone.

I bowed low, the strap pulling tight on my shoulder, and the note was still in my head.

The day had been long. Races. Forms. Lions. Parades. Sweat and worry and running till my lungs burned. But here, in the final glow of sunset, the music made it worth every step.

The festival wasn't just ending, it was soaring.

And somewhere in the back of my mind, I swear I heard the Old Monk chuckle:

"The dragon does not breathe fire at the end of the day. It sings."

Chapter 60

The Text

That evening was the first chance I had to actually see Riley's song.

I'd been there, of course, I'd heard the end of it from the dock, and I'd seen her on stage when I finally made it, but until I watched Mom's video later, I didn't understand just how special it really was. The way Riley stood alone with her guitar, the way her voice carried over thousands of people… it was raw and strong and, honestly, kind of breathtaking.

After my set, I had run down into the crowd to see everyone. Dad was there, and I hugged him so hard it probably knocked some air out of him. I asked what happened, how he'd even made it. He told me the star got sick, the tour was canceled, and Japan would be rescheduled for next year. "Worked out alright, didn't it?" he said with a grin.

I introduced him to Riley, and even Dad seemed impressed, though he tried to play it cool.

Then I found Meiling, the woman who had trusted me with her father's pipa. I tried to hand it back, but she shook her head, eyes already brimming with tears. "No," she said softly. "It was so beautiful tonight. My father would want you to have it. That instrument was made to be played, just like we all heard."Her voice cracked on the last words, and I couldn't say anything for a second. I just nodded, clutching the pipa a little tighter.

I looked around for Arthur, hoping to catch his reaction, but he must have slipped out. I figured I'd hear his thoughts Monday night at my lesson.

With the Kung Fu team, we gathered up all our performance gear, the sashes, the lion heads, the props, and congratulated each other for surviving the day. Third place in the Dragon Boat race. Later I found out it was technically "third place in the second grouping," but whatever. I'll take it.

That night we all went out for dumplings, Sifu, teammates, family, Riley, and filled two long tables. We laughed, teased each other, replayed the best and worst moments, and celebrated until the restaurant had to remind us they were closing.

It wasn't until I was back in my room, the day finally slowing down, that I watched Mom's video again. Riley, standing alone with her guitar, her voice clear but full of ache. Watching her, I felt this weird twist in my chest, like my stomach and throat had both gotten tangled up. My eyes felt funny too, and I had to blink fast.

That's when the Old Monk spoke up, quiet but sharp: *"Ah… music can break your heart, but sometimes it is the musician who does it."*

I groaned and buried my face in my pillow. "Seriously? Now?"

The Monk chuckled. *"Your eyes sting, your chest tightens. You say this is strange. I say… it is only a song of the heart."*

I picked up my phone before he could get another word in.

I just watched your song. It was beautiful. Thank you.

I stared at the screen, hit send, then tossed the phone onto the bed like it might burn me.

The next day at lunch, Riley and I didn't say much. We both seemed kind of wrung out, like the emotion of it all had finally caught up. We sat side by side, eating in quiet relief.

Finally, I asked, "So… are you set for our practice with Jeff?"

"Yes," she said, looking at me with that same calm smile she'd had on stage. "I think we're good."

I swallowed hard, because there it was again, that funny feeling.

Chapter 61

The Quiet Week

The week that followed was quiet, or at least it felt that way compared to the whirlwind of the Dragon Boat Festival. After so much noise, running, and stage lights, even regular school hallways seemed calm.

Arthur gave me a high five when I walked into Rock House for my lesson Monday night. "Kid, that was a show," he said. He didn't even need to mention the pipa. The look in his eyes told me he'd seen enough. Then we dug straight into finalizing riffs for the end-of-season performance this weekend. The notes were sharp, clean, and for once my fingers actually felt ahead of my brain. Progress.

At school, the pumpkins and squash in gardening class were swelling bigger every day, stretching across the soil like they owned the place. Give them another two weeks and they'd be Halloween size, easy. There was something satisfying about watching them grow, slow and steady, while the rest of life spun at high speed.

In Texas History, we'd moved on to the Texas Rangers. Not the baseball team, but the real ones, the lawmen from the 1800s who rode across endless plains, chasing bandits and protecting settlers. Our teacher painted them as half-heroes, half-controversial figures, more complicated than the cowboy movies made them out to be. They had grit, sure, but they also had shadows. Hearing the stories made me imagine galloping across Texas with nothing but a horse, a badge, and an endless horizon. Somehow it reminded me of the blues: tough, raw, full of both pride and pain.

Kung Fu was back to the basics, kicking, punching, running forms over and over. With the Dragon Boat Festival behind us, Sifu pushed us harder on precision. No drums, no parades, no crowds. Just sweat, shouts, and the rhythm of fists cutting the air. I didn't mind. The repetition was grounding, like clearing my head one stance at a time.

Wednesday night at Rock House, Jeff sat back in his chair with his arms folded. He didn't quite smile, but he didn't yell either. For Jeff, that was practically a standing ovation. Riley was electric, her confidence still glowing from her performance at the festival. When she played, it wasn't just music, it was momentum.

And somehow, when we played together, everything clicked. Our parts locked in, like synchronized gears or maybe like breathing. Harmonized. Connected. Whatever it was, it pulled the rest of the band up with us. Colt, Jett, Max and Riley, it felt like, finally, we weren't just practicing. We were a band.

Even sparring Friday night felt lighter. Sid and I still traded kicks and punches, but there was more laughter than bruises, more learning than frustration. The whole class carried an ease, like the pressure valve had finally been released.

By Sunday, I realized how far we'd come. Months ago, when we'd left Oceanside for Twin Lakes, everything felt unsettled, new school, new town, new people, new everything. But now? Sitting in my room with my guitar leaned against one wall and the pipa against the other, it didn't feel new anymore. It felt like mine.

The weekend had been the culmination of everything, the races, the performances, the risks. But this quiet week, in its own way, mattered just as much.

Because this was the week I noticed that life in Twin Lakes wasn't something I was just surviving anymore. It was something I was living.

Chapter 62

TT's

TT's was humming. Plates of sizzling fajitas slid through the crowd. A neon taco blinked above the bar. Families, teachers, kids, regulars, even a couple of kitchen guys still in aprons had drifted toward the stage. The younger bands had done their sets and earned every high five. Now it was our slot, the last one.

We took our places. Amps warmed. Cymbals breathed. Jeff stood with arms crossed near the back. Allison hovered by the soundboard, eyes on us.

Riley stepped to the mic and let the room settle. She didn't rush. She waited for quiet the way a good song waits for the beat to land. Then she spoke.

"Before there was rock," she said, "there was the blues. People took hard days and turned them into sound. That sound crossed rivers and highways, found new cities, found guitars with louder voices. Tonight we are not just playing songs. We are tracing a map. We will start at the roots and follow the roads."

She glanced at us. We were ready.

"Listen for the story."

Colt clicked once. Not four. Just one. Like a heartbeat waking up.

I. Cross Road Blues → Crossroads

I opened alone. No band behind me. Just a small amp and a glass slide on my finger. The room went still. I let space breathe between notes, the way Robert Johnson did, letting the silence talk back. Riley came in soft, not copying anyone, just telling the story like she had found it on a night road.

On the last line she stepped back. Colt lifted brushes to heads. Jett eased into a low pulse. The groove thickened, then snapped tight. I switched the slide for a hard pick, hit the riff, and the room felt it. Cream. Same bones, bigger body. Colt dropped the brushes for sticks. Riley's right hand locked with mine and pushed the tempo a hair, not too much, just enough to feel the floor move.

People didn't scream. They nodded. They leaned forward. The cooks in the pass-through stopped to listen. Jeff's head tilted. He was counting subdivisions. He couldn't help it.

II. The Thrill Is Gone → Since I've Been Loving You

Riley took center. We dimmed the lights a notch. She didn't sing loud. She sang close. B.B. King's melody is a straight line through the heart if you respect it, so we left it clean. Colt used sticks on the rims, a soft click like a clock in a quiet room. Jett walked his line without rushing. I colored the edges with tremolo that shook like a held breath.

Second verse, I bent a note and held it. That's all. Held it until it ached, then let it fall. Someone in back whispered, "Whoa," not because it was fancy, but because we didn't cover it in extras. You could hear the wood and wire.

We shifted almost without a seam. Riley looked once at me, and I knew: now. I leaned into the slow burn, Page's world, same pain, different clothes. The chords climbed like stairs in the dark. Colt's snare cracked once, careful, like lightning far away. We never ran. We didn't need to. We let it rise until her voice opened and the guitar answered and the room forgot to eat.

III. Hoochie Coochie Man → Honky Tonk Women

Time to grin. We did not make it cute. We made it heavy. Jett started the riff with both hands, fat and human. Colt sat behind it like a train. I raked the strings near the bridge for that rough edge. Riley talked more than sang on the first pass, playing with the swagger without winking at it. People laughed and clapped on two and four. Shoulders loosened. Napkins waved.

We pivoted into the Stones by flipping the groove under the same energy. I hit the opening figure bright and dry. Riley found the pocket and rode it. May whooped from our table, and half the room did too. My dad tapped his glass on the table in time. I saw Allison's eyes flicker. She knew exactly what we had done: same attitude, new street.

IV. Smokestack Lightning → Voodoo Child (Slight Return)

We brought the lights down one more notch. Colt rolled the toms low, a ground rumble. I set the tremolo to a slow wobble and fretted the smokestack riff with my palm slightly muting the strings, so it sounded like something alive under a lid. Riley didn't crowd it. She let phrases float over the top and vanish. The room swayed without moving.

Then I stepped on the wah. Not a scream. A murmur that grew. Jett planted a simple, stubborn root. Colt opened the hi-hat and let air in. I shaped the first Voodoo Child phrase like a question. The second phrase answered. Call and response, the same way the blues taught us. When the break came, I cut the volume to almost nothing and let my right hand tremble a single note until you could hear forks clink, then brought the full band back in on a cue only we knew was coming.

It landed. Clean.

I did not chase a thousand notes. I chose a few and made them mean something. Riley doubled my last line an octave down on rhythm guitar, then stepped forward and laid a final chord flat, strong and sure. We stopped together. No ring-out. Silence like a picture frame.

For a second nobody moved.

Then the sound came back.

It wasn't a roar. It was a rise. Chairs scraped, hands clapped, whistles curled up from the back, and people stood because they wanted to, not because anyone told them to. The kitchen window filled with faces. A server in an apron wiped her eye and laughed at herself. My mom pressed a napkin to her cheek. My dad didn't say a word. He just nodded, once, proud, like he does when the take was good.

Allison blew out a breath, then clapped above her head. Jeff didn't smile. He pressed his lips together, tilted his chin, and tapped his heart twice with his knuckles. That was better than a smile.

We bowed. Not perfect. Together.

Riley leaned to the mic, breathless but clear. "Thank you for listening. Thank you to the ones who built these songs. We did our best to carry them."

TT's felt different for a moment. A taco place, yes. But also a little museum, a little church, a little radio station from another time. People went back to talking, ordering, laughing. But softer, like they didn't want to break the air.

We packed our cables slow. Jett hugged his bass. Colt twirled a stick, then caught it and tucked it behind his ear like a pencil. Riley bumped my shoulder with hers and didn't look away.

Somewhere inside, the Old Monk cleared his throat, pleased.

"Bodhi gets the Blues," he said. "And then he got a whole lot more."

The End

"Smaller Than the Tide"

Song By Riley

Verse 1

I was standing by the water
Where the cliffs rise high and steep,
Waves were rolling in forever,
Secrets only oceans keep.

Pre-Chorus

And I wondered if I mattered,
Or if I could just fade away.
But the tide kept on returning,
Like it had something to say.

Chorus

I'm smaller than the tide,
But I'm still here, I'm alive.
Every wave that knocks me down
Teaches me how to survive.
I'm smaller than the tide,
But I'm stronger than the fear.
If the ocean sings forever,
Then I know I'm meant to be here.

Verse 2

Sometimes life can feel like thunder,
Storms that shake you to the bone.
But the stars still burn above us,
Even when we feel alone.

Pre-Chorus
So I'll listen to the silence,
And the song beneath the spray,
'Cause the ocean's voice reminds me,
That the dark won't wash away.

Chorus
I'm smaller than the tide,
But I'm still here, I'm alive.
Every wave that knocks me down
Teaches me how to survive.
I'm smaller than the tide,
But I'm stronger than the fear.
If the ocean sings forever,
Then I know I'm meant to be here.

Bridge
The waves don't ask permission,
They just crash and then they rise.
But I've got my own rhythm,
Like the fire in the skies.

Final Chorus (softer, then building)
I'm smaller than the tide,
But I'm still here, I'm alive.
Every wave that knocks me down
Teaches me how to survive.
I'm smaller than the tide,
But I'm stronger than the fear.
If the ocean sings forever…
Then I know I'm meant to be here.

References

Discography

- Fleetwood Mac. "Rhiannon." Written by Stevie Nicks. *Fleetwood Mac,* Reprise Records, 1975.
- Robert Johnson. "Cross Road Blues." Written by Robert Johnson. Vocalion Records, 1936.
- Robert Johnson. "I Believe I'll Dust My Broom." Written by Robert Johnson. Vocalion Records, 1936.
- Bessie Smith. "St. Louis Blues." Written by W. C. Handy. Columbia Records, 1925.
- Elmore James. "Dust My Broom." Written by Robert Johnson. Flair Records, 1951.
- Muddy Waters. "Mannish Boy." Written by McKinley Morganfield, Ellas McDaniel, and Mel London. *Hard Again,* Blue Sky Records, 1977.
- Muddy Waters. "Hoochie Coochie Man." Written by Willie Dixon. Chess Records, 1954.
- Muddy Waters. "I Just Want to Make Love to You." Written by Willie Dixon. Chess Records, 1954.
- Muddy Waters. "Got My Mojo Working." Written by Preston Foster. Chess Records, 1957.
- Muddy Waters. "Rollin' Stone." Written by McKinley Morganfield. Chess Records, 1950.
- Led Zeppelin. "You Shook Me." Written by Willie Dixon. *Led Zeppelin,* Atlantic Records, 1969.

- Howlin' Wolf. "Smokestack Lightning." Written by Chester Burnett. Chess Records, 1956.
- B. B. King. "The Thrill Is Gone." Written by Roy Hawkins and Rick Darnell. *Completely Well,* Bluesway Records, 1969.
- Cream. "Sunshine of Your Love." Written by Jack Bruce, Eric Clapton, and Pete Brown. *Disraeli Gears,* Reaction Records, 1967.
- The Rolling Stones. "Love in Vain." Written by Robert Johnson. *Let It Bleed,* Decca Records, 1969.
- Jimi Hendrix. "Purple Haze." Written by Jimi Hendrix. *Are You Experienced,* Track Records, 1967.
- **Green Day.** "Basket Case." Written by Billie Joe Armstrong, Mike Dirnt, and Tré Cool. *Dookie,* Reprise Records, 1994.
- Queen. "Bohemian Rhapsody." Written by Freddie Mercury. *A Night at the Opera,* EMI, 1975.
- The Beatles. "While My Guitar Gently Weeps." Written by George Harrison. The Beatles, Apple Records, 1968.

Blues & Rock Musicians / Bands

- B.B. King. *King of the Blues: The Rise and Reign of B.B. King.* Smithsonian Books, 1996.
- Muddy Waters. Gordon, Robert. *Can't Be Satisfied: The Life and Times of Muddy Waters.*Little, Brown, 2002.
- Howlin' Wolf. Segrest, James, and Mark Hoffman. *Moanin' at Midnight: The Life and Times of Howlin' Wolf.* Pantheon, 2004.
- Robert Johnson. Wald, Elijah. *Escaping the Delta: Robert Johnson and the Invention of the Blues.* Amistad, 2004.

- John Lee Hooker. Murray, Charles Shaar. *Boogie Man: The Adventures of John Lee Hooker in the American Twentieth Century.* St. Martin's Press, 2000.
- Eric Clapton. Clapton, Eric. *Clapton: The Autobiography.* Broadway Books, 2007.
- Jimi Hendrix. Cross, Charles R. *Room Full of Mirrors: A Biography of Jimi Hendrix.*Hyperion, 2005.
- Led Zeppelin. Lewis, Dave. *Led Zeppelin: A Celebration.* Omnibus Press, 1991.
- Cream. Welch, Chris. *Cream: The World's First Supergroup.* Backbeat Books, 2000.
- The Rolling Stones. Norman, Philip. *The Stones: The Definitive Biography.* Pan Macmillan, 2012.
- Simple Minds. Thomson, Graeme. *Themes for Great Cities: A New History of Simple Minds.* Omnibus Press, 2022.
- The Cure. O'Donnell, Mick. *Ten Imaginary Years.* Zomba Books, 1988.
- Duran Duran. Nefer, Stephen. *Duran Duran: The First Four Years of the Fab Five.*Omnibus Press, 1984.
- INXS. Waller, Toby Creswell. *INXS: Story to Story.* HarperCollins, 2005.
- U2. Stokes, Niall. *Into the Heart: The Stories Behind Every U2 Song.* Da Capo Press, 2005.
- R.E.M. Gray, Marcus. *It Crawled from the South: An R.E.M. Companion.* Da Capo Press, 1997.
- Oasis. Harris, John. *Britpop!: Cool Britannia and the Spectacular Demise of English Rock.*Da Capo Press, 2004.
- Nirvana. Azerrad, Michael. *Come As You Are: The Story of Nirvana.* Doubleday, 1993.

- Prince. The Beautiful Ones. Spiegel & Grau, 2019.
- Greene, Joshua M. Here Comes the Sun: The Spiritual and Musical Journey of George Harrison. Wiley, 2006.
- Zanes, Warren. Petty: The Biography. Henry Holt, 2015.
- The Beatles. The Beatles Anthology. Chronicle Books, 2000.
- Pearl Jam. Cross, Charles R. *Heavier Than Heaven: The Biography of Kurt Cobain.*Hyperion, 2001..

Blues History & Cultural Context

- Gioia, Ted. *Delta Blues: The Life and Times of the Mississippi Masters Who Revolutionized American Music.* W.W. Norton, 2008.
- Oliver, Paul. *The Story of the Blues.* Northeastern University Press, 1998.
- Ferris, Jean. *America's Musical Landscape.* McGraw Hill, 2007.

Bibliography, Music (Alphabetical by author)

- Azerrad, Michael. *Come As You Are: The Story of Nirvana.* Doubleday, 1993.
- The Beatles. *The Beatles Anthology.* Chronicle Books, 2000.
- Clapton, Eric. *Clapton: The Autobiography.* Broadway Books, 2007.
- Cross, Charles R. *Heavier Than Heaven: The Biography of Kurt Cobain.* Hyperion, 2001.

- Cross, Charles R. *Room Full of Mirrors: A Biography of Jimi Hendrix.* Hyperion, 2005.
- Ferris, Jean. *America's Musical Landscape.* McGraw Hill, 2007.
- Friedlander, Paul. *Rock and Roll: An American History.* Westview Press, 2006.
- Gioia, Ted. *Delta Blues: The Life and Times of the Mississippi Masters Who Revolutionized American Music.* W.W. Norton, 2008.
- Gordon, Robert. *Can't Be Satisfied: The Life and Times of Muddy Waters.* Little, Brown, 2002.
- Gray, Marcus. *It Crawled from the South: An R.E.M. Companion.* Da Capo Press, 1997.
- Greene, Joshua M. *Here Comes the Sun: The Spiritual and Musical Journey of George Harrison.* Wiley, 2006.
- Harris, John. *Britpop!: Cool Britannia and the Spectacular Demise of English Rock.* Da Capo Press, 2004.
- Lewis, Dave. *Led Zeppelin: A Celebration.* Omnibus Press, 1991.
- Light, Alan. *Let's Go Crazy: Prince and the Making of Purple Rain.* Atria Books, 2014.
- Myers, Walter Dean. *Blues Journey.* Illustrated by Christopher Myers, Holiday House, 2003.
- Murray, Charles Shaar. *Boogie Man: The Adventures of John Lee Hooker in the American Twentieth Century.* St. Martin's Press, 2000.
- Nefer, Stephen. *Duran Duran: The First Four Years of the Fab Five.* Omnibus Press, 1984.
- Norman, Philip. *The Stones: The Definitive Biography.* Pan Macmillan, 2012.

- O'Donnell, Mick. *Ten Imaginary Years.* Zomba Books, 1988.
- Oliver, Paul. *The Story of the Blues.* Northeastern University Press, 1998.
- Prince, Prince. *The Beautiful Ones.* Spiegel & Grau, 2019.
- Segrest, James, and Mark Hoffman. *Moanin' at Midnight: The Life and Times of Howlin' Wolf.* Pantheon, 2004.
- Stokes, Niall. *Into the Heart: The Stories Behind Every U2 Song.* Da Capo Press, 2005.
- Thomson, Graeme. *Themes for Great Cities: A New History of Simple Minds.* Omnibus Press, 2022.
- Waller, Toby Creswell. *INXS: Story to Story.* HarperCollins, 2005.
- Wald, Elijah. *Escaping the Delta: Robert Johnson and the Invention of the Blues.* Amistad, 2004.
- Welch, Chris. *Cream: The World's First Supergroup.* Backbeat Books, 2000.
- Zanes, Warren. *Petty: The Biography.* Henry Holt, 2015

Pipa & Chinese Classical Music

- Wu Man – *Immeasurable Light.* Naxos, 2010.
- Liu Fang – *Chinese Pipa Master.* Oliver Sudden Productions, 2001.
- *Ambush from Ten Sides (Shi Mian Mai Fu).* Traditional pipa composition, various performances (notably by Liu Dehai and Wu Man).
- Chen Ziming – *The Pipa: Chinese Lute Music of the Past and Present.* Shanghai Music Publishing, 1989.

Cultural Context

- Wong, Isabel K. F. *Pipa.* Grove Music Online. Oxford University Press.
- Jones, Stephen. *Folk Music of China: Living Instrumental Traditions.* Oxford University Press, 1995.
- Wong, Deborah. *Sounding the Center: History and Aesthetics in Thai Buddhist Ritual.* University of Chicago Press, 2001.
- Nettl, Bruno. *The Study of Ethnomusicology.* University of Illinois Press, 2005.

Further Reading & Listening

Blues Legends

• *Muddy Waters,* Try "Mannish Boy." Loud, raw, powerful.

• *Robert Johnson,* "Cross Road Blues." People say he made a deal with the devil. Creepy but amazing.

• *B.B. King,* "The Thrill Is Gone." Smooth guitar that talks right to your heart.

• *Howlin' Wolf,* "Smokestack Lightning." Growl included.

Rock Bands That Grew From the Blues

• *Led Zeppelin,* "You Shook Me." They took old blues and made it thunder.

• *Cream,* "Sunshine of Your Love." Clapton's riffs live forever.

• *The Rolling Stones,* "Love in Vain." Straight-up blues cover, Stones style.

Bibliography

- Lee, Harper. To Kill a Mockingbird. J. B. Lippincott & Co., 1960.
- Steinbeck, John. Of Mice and Men. Covici Friede, 1937.
- Taylor, Mildred D. Roll of Thunder, Hear My Cry. Dial Press, 1976.
- Hinton, S. E. The Outsiders. Viking Press, 1967.

Children's Literature

- Gutman, Dan. *My Weird School.* HarperCollins, 2004.
- Pilkey, Dav. *Captain Underpants.* Scholastic, 1997.
- Pilkey, Dav. *Dog Man.* Scholastic, 2016.
- Walliams, David. *The World's Worst Children.* HarperCollins, 2016.

Kung Fu References and Resources

The moves in this story were inspired by martial arts traditions. Some draw on classic Kung Fu styles, while others were created just for Bodhi's journey.

Books and Reading

- *Kung Fu for Kids* by Paul Eng, a clear, age-friendly introduction.
- *The Shaolin Way: 10 Modern Secrets of Survival from a Shaolin Grandmaster* by Steve DeMasco, stories and lessons from a Shaolin teacher.
- *Kung Fu Elements* by Paul Dong, explores the history and philosophy of Kung Fu.

Online Resources

- Many martial arts schools share free videos on basics and stances.
- Museums and cultural centers sometimes host exhibits or workshops on Chinese martial arts.

Most Important

Books and videos can inspire you, but nothing replaces real teaching. If Kung Fu interests you, reach out to a **local school or martial arts studio**. Ask to watch a class and see if it feels like a good fit. A good school will welcome beginners, encourage questions, and emphasize respect, safety, and fun.

Remember: Bodhi's journey is a story, but your journey can be real. Every kick, block, and stance is a step toward focus, strength, and confidence.

Chinese Culture
References and Resources

This story includes elements of Chinese culture, history, and traditions, such as food, language, festivals, and music. These details are presented to celebrate the richness of Chinese heritage. Some descriptions are simplified or adapted for storytelling, and readers are encouraged to learn more from authentic sources.

Festivals and Traditions

- **Dragon Boat Festival (Duanwu Jie)**: Celebrated in early summer, this holiday honors the poet Qu Yuan and features dragon boat races and sticky rice dumplings called *zongzi*.
- **Lunar New Year**: The most widely celebrated Chinese holiday, marked by family gatherings, food, red envelopes, and lion or dragon dances.

Food and Eating

- **Rice**: A staple of Chinese meals and a symbol of family and community.
- **Crunchy Rice** (*guōbā*): The crispy rice from the bottom of the pot, enjoyed in both Chinese and Korean cuisines.
- **Dumplings and Noodles**: Common festive foods with regional variations and symbolic meanings.

Music and Instruments

- **Pipa**: Sometimes called the "Chinese guitar," this pear-shaped, four-stringed instrument has been played for over 2,000 years.
- **Erhu**: A two-stringed bowed instrument with a soulful, violin-like sound.

- **Guqin**: A seven-string zither associated with scholars, meditation, and poetry.

Chinese- Traditional

- Traditional. "Shi Mian Mai Fu [Ambush from Ten Sides]." Pipa solo.
- Cal Performances. "Program Notes: Shi Mian Mai Fu (Ambush from Ten Sides)." Program notes for Wu Man, pipa. January 26, 2014. PDF.
- Smithsonian Center for Folklife and Cultural Heritage. "Master of the Chinese Pipa: Wu Man." Program notes for "Shi Mian Mai Fu (Ambush Laid on Ten Sides)." Accessed September 20, 2025.

Books and Reading

- *Moonbeams, Dumplings & Dragon Boats: A Treasury of Chinese Holiday Tales, Activities & Recipes* by Nina Simonds and Leslie Swartz, stories and crafts for kids.
- *The Everything Kids' Learning Mandarin Book* by Jane Wightwick, a fun introduction to Chinese language.
- *Celebrating Chinese Festivals* by Sanmu Tang, an illustrated guide to major holidays and traditions.

Guidance for Students and Families

The traditions described in this book represent only a small glimpse of the richness of Chinese culture. Every region and family may celebrate differently. To learn more, consider:

- Visiting local Chinese cultural centers or museums.
- Attending a Dragon Boat Festival, Lunar New Year, or other community celebrations.
- Exploring Chinese music through live performances or recordings.

This story is a work of fiction. Real traditions are living, diverse, and practiced with care. Exploring them through family, community, and cultural organizations is the best way to honor and appreciate their depth.

Buddhism
References and Resources

This story includes Buddhist ideas such as mindfulness, compassion, and meditation. These are presented in a simplified way for young readers and woven into Bodhi's journey. The tradition of Aumé-Buddhism mentioned in the story is fictional, created only for this book.

Key Ideas in Buddhism

- Mindfulness: Paying attention to the present moment with kindness and focus.
- Compassion: Caring for others and wishing them well.
- The Middle Way: Avoiding extremes and seeking balance in life.
- Meditation: A practice of stillness and awareness that helps calm the mind.

Books and Reading

By Anand Am Reet

- *The Himalayan,* Mirror Lake coming of age story and adventure within Buddhist traditions.
- *The Himalayan for Young Buddhas, Truths, Stories, and Songs,* an age-appropriate introduction to Buddhist stories and practices, a collection of tales and verses that carry Buddhist lessons.

Other Recommended Reading

- *Buddhism for Kids* by Emily Griffith Burke, a gentle introduction for young readers.

- *What Is Buddhism?* by Thubten Chodron, clear answers to common questions.
- *Buddha at Bedtime* by Dharmachari Nagaraja, stories inspired by Buddhist teachings.

Online and Community Resources

- Local meditation centers or Buddhist temples often welcome visitors and offer introductory programs.
- Aume-Buddhism.org, additional resources about the Aumé-Buddhism tradition from this story.
- *Plum Village* (founded by Thích Nhất Hạnh) and the *Buddhist Society*, accessible resources for learning more about mindfulness and Buddhist practice.

Curious about our names, Bodhi and Siddhartha? Read about the Bodhi Tree and the Buddha's journey to enlightenment.

Guidance for Students and Families

Buddhism is a living, global tradition with many schools and practices. The details in this story are not meant to teach Buddhism in full, but to inspire curiosity. The best way to learn more is to explore trusted books, attend cultural or temple events, and speak with knowledgeable teachers.

Authors Bio

Anand Am Reet is an author whose work spans playful fiction for young readers and contemplative books for adults, including *The Himalayan, Mirror Lake.*

Drawing from Buddhist teachings, spiritual practice, and everyday experience, his writing is part of an ongoing exploration of Aumé-Buddhism, a path of mindfulness, creativity, and compassion.

Also By Anand Am Reet

The Himalayan, Mirror Lake

Set among high trails, whispering prayer wheels, and a village at the foot of a monastery, this tale brings Buddhist wisdom into the present, and the Spirit into your every moment.

At the heart of the story is a boy on a journey to see the Great Buddha. Guided by a Buddhist activist who has witnessed exile and the quiet bravery of monks, he enters a world where truth is carried in songs, silence, and the laughter of students. In a village above the clouds, he discovers a love that endures, and a calling that will shape him into a teacher. What begins as a pilgrimage becomes the awakening of a teacher, and something more: a reminder that even in a changing world, truth walks with those who dare to seek it.

The Himalayan for Young Buddhas is a beautifully illustrated collection of stories, poems, and songs that help children build mindfulness, kindness, and inner calm. From playful robot adventures and gentle pony bedtime stories to lyrical verses about compassion and gratitude, this book invites young readers into curiosity, peace, and joyful learning.

Blending timeless Buddhist insights with fun, age-appropriate storytelling, each piece offers children a way to practice patience, share kindness, and grow in awareness. Parents and educators will find it a perfect bedtime companion, teaching values while helping kids settle down with calm, gentle stories.

Proceeds from all Anand Am Reet books support Aumé-Buddhism, a nonprofit dedicated to teaching, publishing, and community service, ensuring that every copy sold contributes to compassion and growth beyond the page.

www.ingramcontent.com/pod-product-compliance
Lightning Source LLC
Chambersburg PA
CBHW020942310726
48980CB00001B/19

* 9 7 9 8 9 9 3 0 5 8 2 4 5 *